WHEN THE MOST IMPORTANT STATESMAN OF THE 21ST CENTURY DISAPPEARS ON MARS

. . . the only hope of preventing interplanetary war lies in a ham actor's ability to impersonate the missing leader well enough to fool two worlds!

Kidnapped from Earth to act the part in this desperate plot, trouper Lorenzo Smythe glories in the performance, despite the risk of assassination if his deception is discovered. But when the vanished politician is secretly found, broken in mind and body, Lorenzo faces a lifetime masquerade—and must choose between causing disaster by quitting, or saving galactic peace by sacrificing his own identity forever.

double star

ROBERT A. HEINLEIN

A SIGNET BOOK from
NEW AMERICAN LIBRARY
TIMES MIRROR

To
Henry
and
Catherine Kuttner

 SIGNET TRADEMARK REG. U.S. PAT. OFF. AND FOREIGN COUNTRIES
REGISTERED TRADEMARK—MARCA REGISTRADA
HECHO EN CHICAGO, U.S.A.

SIGNET, SIGNET CLASSICS, MENTOR, PLUME, MERIDIAN AND NAL
BOOKS are published by The New American Library, Inc.,
1633 Broadway, New York, New York 10019

FIRST SIGNET PRINTING, OCTOBER, 1957

19   20   21   22   23   24   25   26   27

PRINTED IN THE UNITED STATES OF AMERICA

1

If a man walks in dressed like a hick and acting as if he owned the place, he's a spaceman.

It is a logical necessity. His profession makes him feel like boss of all creation; when he sets foot dirtside he is slumming among the peasants. As for his sartorial inelegance, a man who is in uniform nine tenths of the time and is more used to deep space than to civilization can hardly be expected to know how to dress properly. He is a sucker for the alleged tailors who swarm around every spaceport peddling "ground outfits."

I could see that this big-boned fellow had been dressed by Omar the Tentmaker—padded shoulders that were too big to start with, shorts cut so that they crawled up his hairy thighs as he sat down, a ruffled chemise that might have looked well on a cow.

But I kept my opinion to myself and bought him a drink with my last half-Imperial, considering it an investment, spacemen being the way they are about money. "Hot jets!" I said as we touched glasses. He gave me a quick glance.

That was my initial mistake in dealing with Dak Broadbent. Instead of answering, "Clear space!" or, "Safe grounding!" as he should have, he looked me over and said softly, "A nice sentiment, but to the wrong man. I've never been out."

That was another good place to keep my mouth shut. Spacemen did not often come to the bar of Casa Mañana; it was not their sort of hotel and it's miles from the port. When one shows up in ground clothes, seeks a dark corner of the bar, and objects to being called a spaceman, that's *his* business. I had picked that spot myself so that I could see without being seen—I owed a little money here and there at the time, nothing important but embarrassing. I should have assumed that he had his reasons, too, and respected them.

But my vocal cords lived their own life, wild and free. "Don't give me that, shipmate," I replied. "If you're a ground

5

hog, I'm Mayor of Tycho City. I'll wager you've done more drinking on Mars," I added, noticing the cautious way he lifted his glass, a dead giveaway of low-gravity habits, "than you've ever done on Earth."

"Keep your voice down!" he cut in without moving his lips. "What makes you sure that I am a *voyageur?* You don't know me."

"Sorry," I said. "You can be anything you like. But I've got eyes. You gave yourself away the minute you walked in."

He said something under his breath. "How?"

"Don't let it worry you. I doubt if anyone else noticed. But I see things other people don't see." I handed him my card, a little smugly perhaps. There is only one Lorenzo Smythe, the One-Man Stock Company. Yes, I'm "The Great Lorenzo"—stereo, canned opera, legit—"Pantomimist and Mimicry Artist Extraordinary."

He read my card and dropped it into a sleeve pocket—which annoyed me; those cards had cost me money—genuine imitation hand engraving. "I see your point," he said quietly, "but what was wrong with the way I behaved?"

"I'll show you," I said. "I'll walk to the door like a ground hog and come back the way you walk. Watch." I did so, making the trip back in a slightly exaggerated version of his walk to allow for his untrained eye—feet sliding softly along the floor as if it were deck plates, weight carried forward and balanced from the hips, hands a trifle forward and clear of the body, ready to grasp.

There are a dozen other details which can't be set down in words; the point is you have to *be* a spaceman when you do it, with a spaceman's alert body and unconscious balance—you have to live it. A city man blunders along on smooth floors all his life, steady floors with Earth-normal gravity, and will trip over a cigarette paper, like as not. Not so a spaceman.

"See what I mean?" I asked, slipping back into my seat.

"I'm afraid I do," he admitted sourly. "Did I walk like that?"

"Yes."

"Hmm . . . Maybe I should take lessons from you."

"You could do worse," I admitted.

He sat there looking me over, then started to speak—changed his mind and wiggled a finger at the bartender to refill our glasses. When the drinks came, he paid for them, drank his, and slid out of his seat all in one smooth motion. "Wait for me," he said quietly.

With a drink he had bought sitting in front of me I could not refuse. Nor did I want to; he interested me. I liked him,

6

even on ten minutes' acquaintance; he was the sort of big ugly-handsome galoot that women go for and men take orders from.

He threaded his way gracefully through the room and passed a table of four Martians near the door. I didn't like Martians. I did not fancy having a thing that looks like a tree trunk topped off by a sun helmet claiming the privileges of a man. I did not like the way they grew pseudo limbs; it reminded me of snakes crawling out of their holes. I did not like the fact that they could look all directions at once without turning their heads—if they had had heads, which of course they don't. And I could not *stand* their smell!

Nobody could accuse me of race prejudice. I didn't care what a man's color, race, or religion was. But men were men, whereas Martians were *things*. They weren't even animals to my way of thinking. I'd rather have had a wart hog around me any day. Permitting them in restaurants and bars used by men struck me as outrageous. But there was the Treaty, of course, so what could I do?

These four had not been there when I came in, or I would have whiffed them. For that matter, they certainly could not have been there a few moments earlier when I had walked to the door and back. Now there they were, standing on their pedestals around a table, pretending to be people. I had not even heard the air conditioning speed up.

The free drink in front of me did not attract me; I simply wanted my host to come back so that I could leave politely. It suddenly occurred to me that he had glanced over that way just before he had left so hastily and I wondered if the Martians had anything to do with it. I looked over at them, trying to see if they were paying attention to our table—but how could you tell what a Martian was looking at or what it was thinking? That was another thing I didn't like about them.

I sat there for several minutes fiddling with my drink and wondering what had happened to my spaceman friend. I had hoped that his hospitality might extend to dinner and, if we became sufficiently *simpatico,* possibly even to a small temporary loan. My other prospects were—I admit it!—slender. The last two times I had tried to call my agent his autosecretary had simply recorded the message, and unless I deposited coins in the door, my room would not open to me that night . . . That was how low my fortunes had ebbed: reduced to sleeping in a coin-operated cubicle.

In the midst of my melancholy ponderings a waiter touched me on the elbow. "Call for you, sir."

"Eh? Very well, friend, will you fetch an instrument to the table?"

7

"Sorry, sir, but I can't transfer it. Booth 12 in the lobby."

"Oh. Thank you," I answered, making it as warm as possible since I was unable to tip him. I swung wide around the Martians as I went out.

I soon saw why the call had not been brought to the table; No. 12 was a maximum-security booth, sight, sound, and scramble. The tank showed no image and did not clear even after the door locked behind me. It remained milky until I sat down and placed my face within pickup, then the opalescent clouds melted away and I found myself looking at my spaceman friend.

"Sorry to walk out on you," he said quickly, "but I was in a hurry. I want you to come at once to Room 2106 of the Eisenhower."

He offered no explanation. The Eisenhower is just as unlikely a hotel for spacemen as Casa Mañana. I could smell trouble. You don't pick up a stranger in a bar and then insist that he come to a hotel room—well, not one of the same sex, at least.

"Why?" I asked.

The spaceman got that look peculiar to men who are used to being obeyed without question; I studied it with professional interest—it's not the same as anger; it is more like a thundercloud just before a storm. Then he got himself in hand and answered quietly, "Lorenzo, there is no time to explain. Are you open to a job?"

"Do you mean a *professional* engagement?" I answered slowly. For a horrid instant I suspected that he was offering me . . . Well, *you* know—a *job*. Thus far I had kept my professional pride intact, despite the slings and arrows of outrageous fortune.

"Oh, professional, of course!" he answered quickly. "This requires the best actor we can get."

I did not let my relief show in my face. It was true that I was ready for *any* professional work—I would gladly have played the balcony in *Romeo and Juliet*—but it does not do to be eager. "What is the nature of the engagement?" I asked. "My calendar is rather full."

He brushed it aside. "I can't explain over the phone. Perhaps you don't know it, but any scrambler circuit can be unscrambled—with the proper equipment. Shag over here fast!"

He was eager; therefore I could afford not to be eager. "Now really," I protested, "what do you think I am? A bellman? Or an untried juvenile anxious for the privilege of carrying a spear? *I* am Lorenzo!" I threw up my chin and looked offended. "What is your offer?"

"Uh . . . Damn it, I *can't* go into it over the phone. How much do you get?"

"Eh? You are asking my professional salary?"

"Yes, yes!"

"For a single appearance? Or by the week? Or an option contract?"

"Uh, never mind. What do you get by the day?"

"My minimum fee for a one-evening date is one hundred Imperials." This was simple truth. Oh, I have been coerced at times into paying some scandalous kickbacks, but the voucher never read less than my proper fee. A man has his standards. I'd rather starve.

"Very well," he answered quickly, "one hundred Imperials in cash, laid in your hand the minute you show up here. But hurry!"

"Eh?" I realized with sudden dismay that I could as easily have said two hundred, or even two fifty. "But I have not agreed to accept the engagement."

"Never mind that! We'll talk it over when you get here. The hundred is yours even if you turn us down. If you accept—well, call it bonus, over and above your salary. Now will you sign off and get over here?"

I bowed. "Certainly, sir. Have patience."

Fortunately the Eisenhower is not too far from the Casa, for I did not even have a minum for tube fare. However, although the art of strolling is almost lost, I savor it—and it gave me time to collect my thoughts. I was no fool; I was aware that when another man is too anxious to force money on one, it is time to examine the cards. for there is almost certainly something illegal, or dangerous, or both, involved in the matter. I was not unduly fussy about legality *qua* legality; I agreed with the Bard that the Law is often an idiot. But in the main I had stayed on the right side of the street.

But presently I realized that I had insufficient facts, so I put it out of my mind, threw my cape over my right shoulder, and strode along, enjoying the mild autumn weather and the rich and varied odors of the metropolis. On arrival I decided to forego the main entrance and took a bounce tube from the sub-basement to the twenty-first floor, I having at the time a vague feeling that this was not the place to let my public recognize me. My *voyageur* friend let me in. "You took long enough," he snapped.

"Indeed?" I let it go at that and looked around me. It was an expensive suite, as I had expected, but it was littered and there were at least a dozen used glasses and as many coffee cups scattered here and there; it took no skill to see that I was merely the latest of many visitors. Sprawled on a couch,

9

scowling at me, was another man, whom I tabbed tentatively as a spaceman. I glanced inquiringly but no introduction was offered.

"Well, you're here, at least. Let's get down to business."

"Surely. Which brings to mind," I added, "there was mention of a bonus, or retainer."

"Oh, yes." He turned to the man on the couch. "Jock, pay him."

"For what?"

"Pay him!"

I now knew which one was boss—although, as I was to learn, there was usually little doubt when Dak Broadbent was in a room. The other fellow stood up quickly, still scowling, and counted out to me a fifty and five tens. I tucked it away casually without checking it and said, "I am at your disposal, gentlemen."

The big man chewed his lip. "First, I want your solemn oath not even to talk in your sleep about this job."

"If my simple word is not good, is my oath better?" I glanced at the smaller man, slouched again on the couch. "I don't believe we have met. I am Lorenzo."

He glanced at me, looked away. My barroom acquaintance said hastily, "Names don't matter in this."

"No? Before my revered father died he made me promise him three things: first, never to mix whisky with anything but water; second, always to ignore anonymous letters; and lastly, never to talk with a stranger who refuses to give his name. Good day, sirs." I turned toward the door, their hundred Imperials warm in my pocket.

"Hold it!" I paused. He went on, "You are perfectly right. My name is——"

"Skipper!"

"Stow it, Jock. I'm Dak Broadbent; that's Jacques Dubois glaring at us. We're both *voyageurs*—master pilots, all classes, any acceleration."

I bowed. "Lorenzo Smythe," I said modestly, "jongleur and artist—care of The Lambs Club." I made a mental note to pay my dues.

"Good. Jock, try smiling for a change. Lorenzo, you agree to keep our business secret?"

"Under the rose. This is a discussion between gentlemen."

"Whether you take the job or not?"

"Whether we reach agreement or not. I am human, but, short of illegal methods of questioning, your confidences are safe with me."

"I am well aware of what neodexocaine will do to a man's forebrain, Lorenzo. We don't expect the impossible."

"Dak," Dubois said urgently, "this is a mistake. We should at least——"

"Shut up, Jock. I want no hypnotists around at this point. Lorenzo, we want you to do an impersonation job. It has to be so perfect that no one—I mean *no one*—will ever know it took place. Can you do that sort of a job?"

I frowned. "The first question is not 'Can I?' but 'Will I?' What are the circumstances?"

"Uh, we'll go into details later. Roughly, it is the ordinary doubling job for a well-known public figure. The difference is that the impersonation will have to be so perfect as to fool people who know him well and must see him close up. It won't be just reviewing a parade from a grandstand, or pinning medals on girl scouts." He looked at me shrewdly. "It will take a real artist."

"No," I said at once.

"Huh? You don't know anything about the job yet. If your conscience is bothering you, let me assure you that you will not be working against the interests of the man you will impersonate—nor against anyone's legitimate interests. This is a job that really needs to be done."

"No."

"Well, for Pete's sake, why? You don't even know how much we will pay."

"Pay is no object," I said firmly. "I am an actor, not a double."

"I don't understand you. There are lots of actors picking up spare money making public appearances for celebrities."

"I regard them as prostitutes, not colleagues. Let me make myself clear. Does an author respect a ghost writer? Would you respect a painter who allowed another man to sign his work—for *money?* Possibly the spirit of the artist is foreign to you, sir, yet perhaps I may put it in terms germane to your own profession. Would you, simply for *money,* be content to pilot a ship while some other man, not possessing your high art, wore the uniform, received the credit, was publicly acclaimed as the Master? Would you?"

Dubois snorted. "How much money?"

Broadbent frowned at him. "I think I understand your objection."

"To the artist, sir, kudos comes first. Money is merely the mundane means whereby he is enabled to create his art."

"Hmm . . . All right, so you won't do it just for money. Would you do it for other reasons? If you felt that it had to be done and you were the only one who could do it successfully?"

"I concede the possibility; I cannot imagine the circumstances."

11

"You won't have to imagine them; we'll explain them to you."

Dubois jumped up off the couch. "Now see here, Dak, you can't——"

"Cut it, Jock! He has to know."

"He doesn't have to know now—and here. And you haven't any right to jeopardize everybody else by telling him. You don't know a thing about him."

"It's a calculated risk." Broadbent turned back to me.

Dubois grabbed his arm, swung him around. "Calculated risk be damned! Dak, I've strung along with you in the past—but this time before I'll let you shoot off your face, well, one or the other of us isn't going to be in any shape to talk."

Broadbent looked startled, then grinned coldly down at Dubois. "Think you're up to it, Jock old son?"

Dubois glared up at him, did not flinch. Broadbent was a head taller and outweighed him by twenty kilos. I found myself for the first time liking Dubois; I am always touched by the gallant audacity of a kitten, the fighting heart of a bantam cock, or the willingness of a little man to die in his tracks rather than knuckle under . . . And, while I did not expect Broadbent to kill him, I did think that I was about to see Dubois used as a dust rag.

I had no thought of interfering. Every man is entitled to elect the time and manner of his own destruction.

I could see tension grow. Then suddenly Broadbent laughed and clapped Dubois on the shoulder. "Good for you, Jock!" He turned to me and said quietly, "Will you excuse us a few moments? My friend and I must make heap big smoke."

The suite was equipped with a hush corner, enclosing the autograph and the phone. Broadbent took Dubois by the arm and led him over there; they stood and talked urgently.

Sometimes such facilities in public places like hotels are not all that they might be; the sound waves fail to cancel out completely. But the Eisenhower is a luxury house and in this case, at least, the equipment worked perfectly; I could see their lips move but I could hear no sound.

But I could indeed see their lips move. Broadbent's face was toward me and Dubois I could glimpse in a wall mirror. When I was performing in my famous mentalist act, I found out why my father had beaten my tail until I learned the silent language of lips—in my mentalist act I always performed in a brightly lighted hall and made use of spectacles which—but never mind; I could read lips.

Dubois was saying: "Dak, you bloody, stupid, unprintable, illegal and highly improbable obscenity, do you want us

12

both to wind up counting rocks on Titan? This conceited pipsqueak will spill his guts."

I almost missed Broadbent's answer. Conceited indeed! Aside from a cold appreciation of my own genius I felt that I was a modest man.

Broadbent: ". . . doesn't matter if the game is crooked when it's the only game in town. Jock, there is nobody else we can use."

Dubois: "All right, then get Doc Scortia over here, hypnotize him, and shoot him the happy juice. But don't tell him the score—not until he's conditioned, not while we are still on dirt."

Broadbent: "Uh, Scortia himself told me that we could not depend on hypno and drugs, not for the performance we need. We've got to have his co-operation, his intelligent co-operation."

Dubois snorted. "What intelligence? Look at him. Ever see a rooster strutting through a barnyard? Sure, he's the right size and shape and his skull looks a good bit like the Chief—but there is nothing behind it. He'll lose his nerve, blow his top, and give the whole thing away. He can't play the part—he's just a ham actor!"

If the immortal Caruso had been charged with singing off key, he could not have been more affronted than I. But I trust I justified my claim to the mantle of Burbage and Booth at that moment; I went on buffing my nails and ignored it—merely noting that I would someday make friend Dubois both laugh and cry within the span of twenty seconds. I waited a few moments more, then stood up and approached the hush corner. When they saw that I intended to enter it, they both shut up. I said quietly, "Never mind, gentlemen, I have changed my mind."

Dubois looked relieved. "You don't want the job."

"I mean that I accept the engagement. You need not make explanations. I have been assured by friend Broadbent that the work is such as not to trouble my conscience—and I trust him. He has assured me that he needs an actor. But the business affairs of the producer are not my concern. I accept."

Dubois looked angry, but shut up. I expected Broadbent to look pleased and relieved; instead he looked worried. "All right," he agreed, "let's get on with it. Lorenzo, I don't know exactly how long we will need you. No more than a few days, I'm certain—and you will be on display only an hour or so once or twice in that time."

"That does not matter as long as I have time to study the role—the impersonation. But approximately how many days will you need me? I should notify my agent."

"Oh no! Don't do that."

"Well—how long? As much as a week?"

"It will be less than that—or we're sunk."

"Eh?"

"Never mind. Will a hundred Imperials a day suit you?"

I hesitated, recalling how easily he had met my minimum just to interview me—and decided this was a time to be gracious. I waved it aside. "Let's not speak of such things. No doubt you will present me with an honorarium consonant with the worth of my performance."

"All right, all right." Broadbent turned away impatiently. "Jock, call the field. Then call Langston and tell him we're starting Plan Mardi Gras. Synchronize with him. Lorenzo . . ." He motioned for me to follow and strode into the bath. He opened a small case and demanded, "Can you do anything with this junk?"

"Junk" it was—the sort of overpriced and unprofessional make-up kit that is sold over the counter to stage-struck youngsters. I stared at it with mild disgust. "Do I understand, sir, that you expect me to start an impersonation *now?* Without time for study?"

"Huh? No, no, no! I want you to change your face—on the outside chance that someone might recognize you as we leave here. That's possible, isn't it?"

I answered stiffly that being recognized in public was a burden that all celebrities were forced to carry. I did not add that it was certain that countless people would recognize The Great Lorenzo in any public place.

"Okay. So change your phiz so it's not yours." He left abruptly.

I sighed and looked over the child's toys he had handed me, no doubt thinking they were the working tools of my profession—grease paints suitable for clowns, reeking spirit gum, crepe hair which seemed to have been raveled from Aunt Maggie's parlor carpet. Not an ounce of Silicoflesh, no electric brushes, no modern amenities of any sort. But a true artist can do wonders with a burnt match, or oddments such as one might find in a kitchen—and his own genius. I arranged the lights and let myself fall into creative reverie.

There are several ways to keep a well-known face from being recognized. The simplest is misdirection. Place a man in uniform and his face is not likely to be noticed—do you recall the *face* of the last policeman you encountered? Could you identify him if you saw him next in mufti? On the same principle is the attention-going special feature. Equip a man with an enormous nose, disfigured perhaps with *acne rosacea;* the vulgar will stare in fascination at the nose itself, the polite will turn away—but neither will see the face.

14

I decided against this primitive maneuver because I judged that my employer wished me not to be noticed at all rather than remembered for an odd feature without being recognized. This is much more difficult; anyone can be conspicuous but it takes real skill not to be noticed. I needed a face as commonplace, as impossible to remember as the true face of the immortal Alec Guinness. Unfortunately my aristocratic features are entirely too distinguished, too handsome —a regrettable handicap for a character actor. As my father used to say, "Larry, you are too damned pretty! If you don't get off your lazy duff and learn the business, you are going to spend fifteen years as a juvenile, under the mistaken impression that you are an actor—then wind up selling candy in the lobby. 'Stupid' and 'pretty' are the two worst vices in show business—and you're *both*."

Then he would take off his belt and stimulate my brain. Father was a practical psychologist and believed that warming the *glutei maximi* with a strap drew excess blood away from a boy's brain. While the theory may have been shaky, the results justified the method; by the time I was fifteen I could stand on my head on a slack wire and quote page after page of Shakespeare and Shaw—or steal a scene simply by lighting a cigarette.

I was deep in the mood of creation when Broadbent stuck his face in. "Good grief!" he snapped. "Haven't you done anything yet?"

I stared coldly. "I assumed that you wanted my best creative work—which cannot be hurried. Would you expect a *cordon bleu* to compound a new sauce on the back of a galloping horse?"

"Horses be damned!" He glanced at his watch finger. "You have six more minutes. If you can't do anything in that length of time, we'll just have to take our chances."

Well! Of course I prefer to have plenty of time—but I had understudied my father in his quick-change creation, *The Assassination of Huey Long,* fifteen parts in seven minutes —and had once played it in nine seconds less time than he did. "Stay where you are!" I snapped back at him. "I'll be with you at once." I then put on "Benny Grey," the colorless handy man who does the murders in *The House with No Doors*—two quick strokes to put dispirited lines into my cheeks from nose to mouth corners, a mere suggestion of bags under my eyes, and Factor's #5 sallow over all, taking not more than twenty seconds for everything—I could have done it in my sleep; *House* ran on boards for ninety-two performances before they recorded it.

Then I faced Broadbent and he gasped. "Good God! I don't believe it."

15

I stayed in "Benny Grey" and did not smile acknowledgment. What Broadbent could not realize was that the grease paint really was not necessary. It makes it easier, of course, but I had used a touch of it primarily because he expected it; being one of the yokels, he naturally assumed that make-up consisted of paint and powder.

He continued to stare at me. "Look here," he said in a hushed voice, "could you do something like that for *me?* In a hurry?"

I was about to say no when I realized that it presented an interesting professional challenge. I had been tempted to say that if my father had started in on him at five he might be ready now to sell cotton candy at a punkin' doin's, but I thought better of it. "You simply want to be sure that you will not be recognized?" I asked.

"Yes, yes! Can you paint me up, or give me a false nose, or something?"

I shook my head. "No matter what we did with make-up, it would simply make you look like a child dressed up for Trick or Treat. You can't act and you can never learn, at your age. We won't touch your face."

"Huh? But with this beak on me——"

"Attend me. Anything I could do to that lordly nose would just call attention to it, I assure you. Would it suffice if an acquaintance looked at you and said, 'Say, that big fellow reminds me of Dak Broadbent. It's not Dak, of course, but looks a little like him.' Eh?"

"Huh? I suppose so. As long as he was sure it wasn't me. I'm supposed to be on . . . Well, I'm not supposed to be on Earth just now."

"He'll be quite sure it is not you, because we'll change your walk. That's the most distinctive thing about you. If your walk is wrong, it cannot possibly be *you*—so it must be some other big-boned, broad-shouldered man who looks a bit like you."

"Okay, show me how to walk."

"No, you could never learn it. I'll force you to walk the way I want you to."

"How?"

"We'll put a handful of pebbles or the equivalent in the toes of your boots. That will force you back on your heels and make you stand up straight. It will be impossible for you to sneak along in that catfooted spaceman's crouch. Mmm . . . I'll slap some tape across your shoulder blades to remind you to keep your shoulders back, too. That will do it."

"You think they won't recognize me just because I'll walk differently?"

"Certain. An acquaintance won't know why he is sure it is not you, but the very fact that the conviction is subconscious and unanalyzed will put it beyond reach of doubt. Oh, I'll do a little something to your face, just to make you feel easier—but it isn't necessary."

We went back into the living room of the suite. I was still being "Benny Grey" of course; once I put on a role it takes a conscious effort of will to go back to being myself. Dubois was busy at the phone; he looked up, saw me, and his jaw dropped. He hurried out of the hush locus and demanded, "Who's *he?* And where's that actor fellow?" After his first glance at me, he had looked away and not bothered to look back—"Benny Grey" is such a tired, negligible little guy that there is no point in looking at him.

"What actor fellow?" I answered in Benny's flat, colorless tones. It brought Dubois' eyes back to me. He looked at me, started to look away, his eyes snapped back, then he looked at my clothes. Broadbent guffawed and clapped him on the shoulder.

"And *you* said he couldn't act!" He added sharply, "Did you get them all, Jock?"

"Yes." Dubois looked back at me, looked perplexed, and looked away.

"Okay. We've got to be out of here in four minutes. Let's see how fast you can get me fixed up, Lorenzo."

Dak had one boot off, his blouse off, and his chemise pulled up so that I could tape his shoulders when the light over the door came on and the buzzer sounded. He froze. "Jock? We expecting anybody?"

"Probably Langston. He said he was going to try to get over here before we left." Dubois started for the door.

"It might not be him. It might be——" I did not get to hear Broadbent say who he thought it might be as Dubois dilated the door. Framed in the doorway, looking like a nightmare toadstool, was a Martian.

For an agony-stretched second I could see nothing but the Martian. I did not see the human standing behind him, nor did I notice the life wand the Martian cradled in his pseudo limb.

Then the Martian flowed inside, the man with him stepped in behind him, and the door relaxed. The Martian squeaked, "Good afternoon, gentlemen. Going somewhere?"

I was frozen, dazed, by acute xenophobia. Dak was handicapped by disarranged clothing. But little Jock Dubois acted with a simple heroism that made him my beloved brother even as he died . . . He flung himself at that life wand. Right at it—he made no attempt to evade it.

He must have been dead, a hole burned through his belly

17

you could poke a fist through, before he hit the floor. But he hung on and the pseudo limb stretched like taffy—then snapped, broken off a few inches from the monster's neck, and poor Jock still had the life wand cradled in his dead arms.

The human who had followed that stinking, reeking thing into the room had to step to one side before he could get in a shot—and he made a mistake. He should have shot Dak first, then me. Instead he wasted his first one on Jock and he never got a second one, as Dak shot him neatly in the face. I had not even known Dak was armed.

Deprived of his weapon, the Martian did not attempt to escape. Dak bounced to his feet, slid up to him, and said, "Ah, Rrringriil. I see you."

"I see you, Captain Dak Broadbent," the Martian squeaked, then added, "You will tell my nest?"

"I will tell your nest, Rrringriil."

"I thank you, Captain Dak Broadbent."

Dak reached out a long bony finger and poked it into the eye nearest him, shoving it on home until his knuckles were jammed against the brain case. He pulled it out and his finger was slimed with green ichor. The creature's pseudo limbs crawled back into its trunk in reflex spasm but the dead thing continued to stand firm on its base. Dak hurried into the bath; I heard him washing his hands. I stayed where I was, almost as frozen by shock as the late Rrringriil.

Dak came out, wiping his hands on his shirt, and said, "We'll have to clean this up. There isn't much time." He could have been speaking of a spilled drink.

I tried to make clear in one jumbled sentence that I wanted no part of it, that we ought to call the cops, that I wanted to get away from there before the cops came, that he knew what he could do with his crazy impersonation job, and that I planned to sprout wings and fly out the window. Dak brushed it all aside. "Don't jitter, Lorenzo. We're on minus minutes now. Help me get the bodies into the bathroom."

"Huh? Good God, man! Let's just lock up and run for it. Maybe they will never connect us with it."

"Probably they wouldn't," he agreed, "since neither one of us is supposed to be here. But they would be able to see that Rrringriil had killed Jock—and we can't have *that*. Not now we can't."

"Huh?"

"We can't afford a news story about a Martian killing a human. So shut up and help me."

I shut up and helped him. It steadied me to recall that "Benny Grey" had been the worst of sadistic psychopaths, who had enjoyed dismembering his victims. I let "Benny Grey" drag the two human bodies into the bath while Dak took the life wand and sliced Rrringriil into pieces small enough to handle. He was careful to make the first cut below the brain case so the job was not messy, but I could not help him with it—it seemed to me that a dead Martian stank even worse than a live one.

The oubliette was concealed in a panel in the bath just beyond the bidet; if it had not been marked with the usual radiation trefoil it would have been hard to find. After we had shoved the chunks of Rrringriil down it (I managed to get my spunk up enough to help), Dak tackled the messier problem of butchering and draining the human corpses, using the wand and, of course, working in the bath tub.

It is amazing how much blood a man holds. We kept the water running the whole time; nevertheless, it was bad. But when Dak had to tackle the remains of poor little Jock, he just wasn't up to it. His eyes flooded with tears, blinding him, so I elbowed him aside before he sliced off his own fingers and let "Benny Grey" take over.

When I had finished and there was nothing left to show that there had ever been two other men and a monster in the suite, I sluiced out the tub carefully and stood up. Dak was in the doorway, looking as calm as ever. "I've made sure the floor is tidy," he announced. "I suppose a criminologist with proper equipment could reconstruct it—but we are counting on no one ever suspecting. So let's get out of here. We've got to gain almost twelve minutes somehow. Come on!"

I was beyond asking where or why. "All right. Let's fix your boots."

He shook his head. "It would slow me up. Right now speed is more essential than not being recognized."

"I am in your hands." I followed him to the door; he stopped and said, "There may be others around. If so, shoot first—there's nothing else you can do." He had the life wand in his hand, with his cloak drawn over it.

"Martians?"

"Or men. Or both."

"Dak? Was Rrringriil one of those four at the Mañana bar?"

"Certainly. Why do you think I went around Robinson's barn to get you out of there and over here? They either tailed you, as we did, or they tailed me. Didn't you recognize him?"

"Heavens, no! Those monsters all look alike to me."

"And *they* say *we* all look alike. The four were Rrringriil, his conjugate-brother Rrringlath, and two others from his nest, of divergent lines. But shut up. If you see a Martian, shoot. You have the other gun?"

"Uh, yes. Look, Dak, I don't know what this is all about.

19

But as long as those beasts are against you, I'm with you. I despise Martians."

He looked shocked. "You don't know what you are saying. We're not fighting Martians; those four are renegades."

"Huh?"

"There are lots of good Martians—almost all of them. Shucks, even Rrringriil wasn't a bad sort in most ways— I've had many a fine chess game with him."

"What? In that case, I'm——"

"Stow it. You're in too deep to back out. Now quick-march, straight to the bounce tube. I'll cover our rear."

I shut up. I was in much too deep—that was unarguable.

We hit the sub-basement and went at once to the express tubes. A two-passenger capsule was just emptying; Dak shoved me in so quickly that I did not see him set the control combination. But I was hardly surprised when the pressure let up from my chest and I saw the sign blinking JEFFERSON SKYPORT—All Out.

Nor did I care what station it was as long as it was as far as possible from Hotel Eisenhower. The few minutes we had been crammed in the vactube had been long enough for me to devise a plan—sketchy, tentative, and subject to change without notice, as the fine print always says, but a plan. It could be stated in two words: Get lost!

Only that morning I would have found the plan very difficult to execute; in our culture a man with no money at all is baby-helpless. But with a hundred slugs in my pocket I could go far and fast. I felt no obligation to Dak Broadbent. For reasons of his own—not *my* reasons!—he had almost got me killed, then had crowded me into covering up a crime, made me a fugitive from justice. But we had evaded the police, temporarily at least, and now, simply by shaking off Broadbent, I could forget the whole thing, shelve it as a bad dream. It seemed most unlikely that I could be connected with the affair even if it were discovered—fortunately a gentleman always wears gloves, and I had had mine off only to put on make-up and later during that ghastly house cleaning.

Aside from the warm burst of adolescent heroics I had felt when I thought Dak was fighting Martians I had no interest in his schemes—and even that sympathy had shut off when I found that he liked Martians in general. His impersonation job I would not now touch with the proverbial eleven-foot pole. To hell with Broadbent! All I wanted out of life was money enough to keep body and soul together and a chance to practice my art; cops-and-robbers nonsense did not interest me—poor theater at best.

Jefferson Port seemed handmade to carry out my scheme.

Crowded and confused, with express tubes spiderwebbing from it, in it, if Dak took his eyes off me for half a second I would be halfway to Omaha. I would lie low a few weeks, then get in touch with my agent and find out if any inquiries had been made about me.

Dak saw to it that we climbed out of the capsule together, else I would have slammed it shut and gone elsewhere at once. I pretended not to notice and stuck close as a puppy to him as we went up the belt to the main hall just under the surface, coming out between the Pan-Am desk and American Skylines. Dak headed straight across the waiting-room floor toward Diana, Ltd., and I surmised that he was going to buy tickets for the Moon shuttle—how he planned to get me aboard without passport or vaccination certificate I could not guess but I knew that he was resourceful. I decided that I would fade into the furniture while he had his wallet out; when a man counts money there are at least a few seconds when his eyes and attention are fully occupied.

But we went right on past the Diana desk and through an archway marked *Private Berths*. The passageway beyond was not crowded and the walls were blank; I realized with dismay that I had let slip my best chance, back there in the busy main hall. I held back. "Dak? Are we making a jump?"

"Of course."

"Dak, you're crazy. I've got no papers, I don't even have a tourist card for the Moon."

"You won't need them."

"Huh? They'll stop me at 'Emigration.' Then a big, beefy cop will start asking questions."

A hand about the size of a cat closed on my upper arm. "Let's not waste time. Why should you go through 'Emigration,' when officially you aren't leaving? And why should I, when officially I never arrived? Quick-march, old son."

I am well muscled and not small, but I felt as if a traffic robot were pulling me out of a danger zone. I saw a sign reading MEN and I made a desperate attempt to break it up. "Dak, half a minute, please. Got to see a man about the plumbing."

He grinned at me. "Oh, yes? You went just before we left the hotel." He did not slow up or let go of me.

"Kidney trouble——"

"Lorenzo old son, I smell a case of cold feet. Tell you what I'll do. See that cop up ahead?" At the end of the corridor, in the private berths station, a defender of the peace was resting his big feet by leaning over a counter. "I find I have a sudden attack of conscience. I feel a need to confess—about how you killed a visiting Martian and two local

21

citizens—about how you held a gun on me and forced me to help you dispose of the bodies. About——"

"You're crazy!"

"Almost out of my mind with anguish and remorse, shipmate."

"But—you've got nothing on me."

"So? I think my story will sound more convincing than yours. I know what it is all about and you don't. I know all about you and you know nothing about me. For example . . ." He mentioned a couple of details in my past that I would have sworn were buried and forgotten. All right, so I did have a couple of routines useful for stag shows that are not for the family trade—a man has to eat. But that matter about Bebe; that was hardly fair, for I certainly had not known that she was underage. As for that hotel bill, while it is true that bilking an "innkeeper" in Miami Beach carries much the same punishment as armed robbery elsewhere, it is a very provincial attitude—I would have paid if I had had the money. As for that unfortunate incident in Seattle—well, what I am trying to say is that Dak did know an amazing amount about my background but he had the wrong slant on most of it. Still . . .

"So," he continued, "let's walk right up to yon gendarme and make a clean breast of it. I'll lay you seven to two as to which one of us is out on bail first."

So we marched up to the cop and on past him. He was talking to a female clerk back of the railing and neither one of them looked up. Dak took out two tickets reading, GATE PASS—MAINTENANCE PERMIT—Berth K-127, and stuck them into the monitor. The machine scanned them, a transparency directed us to take an upper-level car, code King 127; the gate let us through and locked behind us as a recorded voice said, "Watch your step, please, and heed radiation warnings. The Terminal Company is not responsible for accidents beyond the gate."

Dak punched an entirely different code in the little car; it wheeled around, picked a track, and we took off out under the field. It did not matter to me, I was beyond caring.

When we stepped out of the little car it went back where it came from. In front of me was a ladder disappearing into the steel ceiling above. Dak nudged me. "Up you go." There was a scuttle hole at the top and on it a sign: RADIATION HAZARD—Optimax 13 Seconds. The figures had been chalked in. I stopped. I have no special interest in offspring but I am no fool. Dak grinned and said, "Got your lead britches on? Open it, go through at once and straight up the ladder into the ship. If you don't stop to scratch, you'll make it with at least three seconds to spare."

I believe I made it with five seconds to spare. I was out in the sunlight for about ten feet, then I was inside a long tube in the ship. I used about every third rung.

The rocket ship was apparently small. At least the control room was quite cramped; I never got a look at the outside. The only other spaceships I had ever been in were the Moon shuttles *Evangeline* and her sister ship the *Gabriel,* that being the year in which I had incautiously accepted a lunar engagement on a co-op basis—our impresario had had a notion that a juggling, tightrope, and acrobatic routine would go well in the one-sixth gee of the Moon, which was correct as far as it went, but he had not allowed rehearsal time for us to get used to low gravity. I had to take advantage of the Distressed Travelers Act to get back and I had lost my wardrobe.

There were two men in the control room; one was lying in one of three acceleration couches fiddling with dials, the other was making obscure motions with a screw driver. The one in the couch glanced at me, said nothing. The other one turned, looked worried, then said past me, "What happened to Jock?"

Dak almost levitated out of the hatch behind me. "No time!" he snapped. "Have you compensated for his mass?"

"Yes."

"Red, is she taped? Tower?"

The man in the couch answered lazily, "I've been recomputing every two minutes. You're clear with the tower. Minus forty-, uh, seven seconds."

"Out of that bunk! Scram! I'm going to catch that tick!"

Red moved lazily out of the couch as Dak got in. The other man shoved me into the copilot's couch and strapped a safety belt across my chest. He turned and dropped down the escape tube. Red followed him, then stopped with his head and shoulders out. "Tickets, please!" he said cheerfully.

"Oh, cripes!" Dak loosened a safety belt, reached for a pocket, got out the two field passes we had used to sneak aboard, and shoved them at him.

"Thanks," Red answered. "See you in church. Hot jets, and so forth." He disappeared with leisurely swiftness; I heard the air lock close and my eardrums popped. Dak did not answer his farewell; his eyes were busy on the computer dials and he made some minor adjustment.

"Twenty-one seconds," he said to me. "There'll be no rundown. Be sure your arms are inside and that you are relaxed. The first step is going to be a honey."

I did as I was told, then waited for *hours* in that curtain-going-up tension. Finally I said, "Dak?"

"Shut up!"

"Just one thing: where are we going?"

"Mars." I saw his thumb jab at a red button and I blacked out.

2

What is so funny about a man being dropsick? Those dolts with cast-iron stomachs always laugh—I'll bet they would laugh if Grandma broke both legs.

I was spacesick, of course, as soon as the rocket ship quit blasting and went into free fall. I came out of it fairly quickly as my stomach was practically empty—I'd eaten nothing since breakfast—and was simply wanly miserable the remaining eternity of that awful trip. It took us an hour and forty-three minutes to make rendezvous, which is roughly equal to a thousand years in purgatory to a ground hog like myself.

I'll say this for Dak, though: he did not laugh. Dak was a professional and he treated my normal reaction with the impersonal good manners of a flight nurse—not like those flat-headed, loud-voiced jackasses you'll find on the passenger list of a Moon shuttle. If I had my way, those healthy self-panickers would be spaced in mid-orbit and allowed to laugh themselves to death in vacuum.

Despite the turmoil in my mind and the thousand questions I wanted to ask we had almost made rendezvous with a torchship, which was in parking orbit around Earth, before I could stir up interest in anything. I suspect that if one were to inform a victim of spacesickness that he was to be shot at sunrise his own answer would be, "Yes? Would you hand me that sack, please?"

But I finally recovered to the point where instead of wanting very badly to die the scale had tipped so that I had a flickering, halfhearted interest in continuing to live. Dak was busy most of the time at the ship's communicator, apparently talking on a very tight beam for his hands constantly nursed the directional control like a gunner laying a gun under difficulties. I could not hear what he said, or even read his lips, as he had his face pushed into the rumble box. I assumed that he was talking to the long-jump ship we were to meet.

But when he pushed the communicator aside and lit a

cigarette I repressed the stomach retch that the mere sight of tobacco smoke had inspired and said, "Dak, isn't it about time you told me the score?"

"Plenty of time for that on our way to Mars."

"Huh? Damn your arrogant ways," I protested feebly. "I don't want to go to Mars. I would never have considered your crazy offer if I had known it was on Mars."

"Suit yourself. You don't have to go."

"Eh?"

"The air lock is right behind you. Get out and walk. Mind you close the door."

I did not answer the ridiculous suggestion. He went on, "But if you can't breathe space the easiest thing to do is to go to Mars—and I'll see that you get back. The *Can Do*—that's this bucket—is about to rendezvous with the *Go For Broke*, which is a high-gee torchship. About seventeen seconds and a gnat's wink after we make contact the *Go For Broke* will torch for Mars—for we've *got* to be there by Wednesday."

I answered with the petulant stubbornness of a sick man. "I'm not going to Mars. I'm going to stay right in this ship. Somebody has to take it back and land it on Earth. You can't fool me."

"True," Broadbent agreed. "But you won't be in it. The three blokes who are supposed to be in this ship—according to the records back at Jefferson Field—are in the *Go For Broke* right now. This is a three-man ship, as you've noticed. I'm afraid you will find them stuffy about giving up a place to you. And besides, how would you get back through 'Immigration'?"

"I don't care! I'd be back on ground."

"And in jail, charged with everything from illegal entry to mopery and dopery in the spaceways. At the very least they would be sure that you were smuggling and they would take you to some quiet back room and run a needle in past your eyeball and find out just what you were up to. They would know what questions to ask and you wouldn't be able to keep from answering. But you wouldn't be able to implicate me, for good old Dak Broadbent hasn't been back to Earth in quite a spell and has unimpeachable witnesses to prove it."

I thought about it sickly, both from fear and the continuing effects of spacesickness. "So you would tip off the police? You dirty, slimy——" I broke off for lack of an adequately insulting noun.

"Oh no! Look, old son, I might twist your arm a bit and let you think that I would cry copper—but I never would. But Rrringriil's conjugate-brother Rrringlath certainly knows that old 'Griil' went in that door and failed to come

25

out. He will tip off the noises. Conjugate-brother is a relation-ship so close that we will never understand it, since we don't reproduce by fission."

I didn't care whether Martians reproduced like rabbits or the stork brought them in a little black bag. The way he told it I could never go back to Earth, and I said so. He shook his head. "Not at all. Leave it to me and we will slide you back in as neatly as we slid you out. Eventually you will walk off that field or some other field with a gate pass which shows that you are a mechanic who has been making some last-minute adjustment—and you'll have greasy cover-alls and a tool kit to back it up. Surely an actor of your skill can play the part of a mechanic for a few minutes?"

"Eh? Why, certainly! But——"

"There you are! You stick with ol' Doc Dak; he'll take care of you. We shuffled eight guild brothers in this current caper to get me on Earth and both of us off; we can do it again. But you would not stand a chance without *voyageurs* to help you." He grinned. "Every *voyageur* is a free trader at heart. The art of smuggling being what it is, we are all of us always ready to help out one another in a little inno-cent deception of the port guards. But a person outside the lodge does not ordinarily get such cooperation."

I tried to steady my stomach and think about it. "Dak, is this a smuggling deal? Because——"

"Oh no! Except that we are smuggling *you*."

"I was going to say that I don't regard smuggling as a crime."

"Who does? Except those who make money off the rest of us by limiting trade. But this is a straight impersonation job, Lorenzo, and you are the man for it. It wasn't an acci-dent that I ran across you in the bar; there had been a tail on you for two days. As soon as I hit dirt I went where you were." He frowned. "I wish I could be sure our honor-able antagonists had been following *me*, and not you."

"Why?"

"If they were following me they were trying to find out what I was after—which is okay, as the lines were already drawn; we knew we were mutual enemies. But if they were following *you*, then they *knew* what I was after—an actor who could play the role."

"But how could they know that? Unless you told them?"

"Lorenzo, this thing is big, much bigger than you imagine. I don't see it all myself—and the less you know about it until you must, the better off you are. But I can tell you this: a set of personal characteristics was fed into the big computer at the System Census Bureau at The Hague and the ma-chine compared them with the personal characteristics of

26

every male professional actor alive. It was done as discreetly as possible but somebody might have guessed—and talked. The specifications amounted to identification both of the principal and the actor who could double for him, since the job had to be *perfect*."

"Oh. And the machine told you that I was the man for it?"

"Yes. You—and one other."

This was another good place for me to keep my mouth shut. But I could not have done so if my life had depended on it—which in a way it did. I just had to know who the other actor was who was considered competent to play a role which called for my unique talents. "This other one? Who is he?"

Dak looked me over; I could see him hesitate. "Mmm—fellow by the name of Orson Trowbridge. Know him?"

"*That* ham!" For a moment I was so furious that I forgot my nausea.

"So? I hear that he is a very good actor."

I simply could not help being indignant at the idea that anyone should even think about that oaf Trowbridge for a role for which I was being considered. "That arm-waver! That word-mouther!" I stopped, realizing that it was more dignified to ignore such colleagues—if the word fits. But that popinjay was so conceited that—well, if the role called for him to kiss a lady's hand, Trowbridge would fake it by kissing his own thumb instead. A narcissist, a poseur, a double fake—how could such a man *live* a role?

Yet such is the injustice of fortune that his sawings and rantings had paid him well while real artists went hungry.

"Dak, I simply cannot see why you considered him for it."

"Well, we didn't want him; he is tied up with some long-term contract that would make his absence conspicuous and awkward. It was lucky for us that you were—uh, 'at liberty.' As soon as you agreed to the job I had Jock send word to call off the team that was trying to arrange a deal with Trowbridge."

"I should think so!"

"But—see here, Lorenzo, I'm going to lay it on the line. While you were busy whooping your cookies after *Brennschluss* I called the *Go For Broke* and told them to pass the word down to get busy on Trowbridge again."

"*What?*"

"You asked for it, shipmate. See here, a man in my racket contracts to herd a heap to Ganymede, that means he will pilot that pot to Ganymede or die trying. He doesn't get fainthearted and try to welsh while the ship is being loaded. You told me you would take this job—no 'ifs' or 'ands' or 'buts'—you took the job. A few minutes later there is a

27

fracas; you lose your nerve. Later you try to run out on me at the field. Only ten minutes ago you were screaming to be taken back dirtside. Maybe you are a better actor than Trowbridge. I wouldn't know. But I know we need a man who can be depended on not to lose his nerve when the time comes. I understand that Trowbridge is that sort of bloke. So if we can get him, we'll use him instead, pay you off and tell you nothing and ship you back. Understand?"

Too well I understood. Dak did not use the word—I doubt if he would have understood it—but he was telling me that I was not a trouper. The bitter part about it was that he was justified. I could not be angry; I could only be ashamed. I had been an idiot to accept the contract without knowing more about it—but I had agreed to play the role, without conditions or escape clauses. Now I was trying to back out, like a rank amateur with stage fright.

"The show must go on" is the oldest tenet of show business. Perhaps it has no philosophical verity, but the things men live by are rarely subject to logical proof. My father had believed it—I had seen him play two acts with a burst appendix and then take his bows before he had let them rush him to a hospital. I could see his face now, looking at me with the contempt of a trouper for a so-called actor who would let an audience down.

"Dak," I said humbly, "I am very sorry. I was wrong."

He looked at me sharply. "You'll do the job?"

"Yes." I meant it sincerely. Then I suddenly remembered a factor which could make the part as impossible for me as the role of Snow White in *The Seven Dwarfs*. "That is—well, *I want* to. But——"

"But what?" he said scornfully. "More of your damned temperament?"

"No, no! But you said we were going to Mars. Dak, am I going to be expected to do this impersonation with Martians around me?"

"Eh? Of course. How else on Mars?"

"Uh . . . But, Dak, I can't *stand* Martians! They give me the heebie jeebies. I wouldn't want to—I would try not to— but I might fall right out of the characterization."

"Oh. If that is all that is worrying you, forget it."

"Huh? But I can't forget it. I can't help it. I——"

"I said, 'Forget it.' Old son, we knew you were a peasant in such matters—we know all about you. Lorenzo, your fear of Martians is as childish and irrational as a fear of spiders or snakes. But we had anticipated it and it will be taken care of. So forget it."

"Well—all right." I was not much reassured, but he had

flicked me where it hurt. "Peasant"—why, *"peasants"* were the audience! So I shut up.

Dak pulled the communicator to him, did not bother to silence his message with the rumble box: "Dandelion to Tumbleweed—cancel Plan Inkblot. We will complete Mardi Gras."

"Dak?" I said as he signed off.

"Later," he answered. "I'm about to match orbits. The contact may be a little rough, as I am not going to waste time worrying about chuck holes. So pipe down and hang on."

And it *was* rough. By the time we were in the torchship I was glad to be comfortably back in free fall again; surge nausea is even worse than everyday dropsickness. But we did not stay in free fall more than five minutes; the three men who were to go back in the *Can Do* were crowding into the transfer lock even as Dak and I floated into the torchship. The next few moments were extremely confused. I suppose I am a ground hog at heart for I disorient very easily when I can't tell the floor from the ceiling. Someone called out, "Where is he?" Dak replied, "Here!" The same voice replied, "Him?" as if he could not believe his eyes.

"Yes, yes!" Dak answered. "He's got make-up on. Never mind, it's all right. Help me get him into the cider press."

A hand grabbed my arm, towed me along a narrow passage and into a compartment. Against one bulkhead and flat to it were two bunks, or "cider presses," the bathtub-shaped, hydraulic, pressure-distribution tanks used for high acceleration in torchships. I had never seen one before but we had used quite convincing mock-ups in the space opus *The Earth Raiders*.

There was a stenciled sign on the bulkhead behind the bunks: *WARNING!!! Do Not Take More than Three Gravities without a Gee Suit. By Order of——* I rotated slowly out of range of vision before I could finish reading it and someone shoved me into one cider press. Dak and the other men were hurriedly strapping me against it when a horn somewhere near by broke into a horrid hooting. It continued for several seconds, then a voice replaced it: "Red warning! Two gravities! Three minutes! Red warning! Two gravities! Three minutes!" Then the hooting started again.

Through the racket I heard Dak ask urgently, "Is the projector all set? The tapes ready?"

"Sure, sure!"

"Got the hypo?" Dak squirmed around in the air and said to me, "Look, shipmate, we're going to give you a shot. It's all right. Part of it is Nullgrav, the rest is a stimulant—for you are going to have to stay awake and study your lines.

It will make your eyeballs feel hot at first and it may make you itch, but it won't hurt you."

"Wait, Dak, I——"

"No time! I've got to smoke this scrap heap!" He twisted and was out the door before I could protest. The second man pushed up my left sleeve, held an injection gun against the skin, and I had received the dose before I knew it. Then he was gone. The hooting gave way to: "Red warning! Two gravities! Two minutes!"

I tried to look around but the drug made me even more confused. My eyeballs did feel hot and my teeth as well and I began to feel an almost intolerable itching along my spine—but the safety straps kept me from reaching the tortured area—and perhaps kept me from breaking an arm at acceleration. The hooting stopped again and this time Dak's self-confident baritone boomed out, "Last red warning! Two gravities! One minute! Knock off those pinochle games and spread your fat carcasses—we're goin' to smoke!" The hooting was replaced this time by a recording of Arkezian's *Ad Astra*, opus 61 in C major. It was the controversial London Symphony version with the 14-cycle "scare" notes buried in the timpani. Battered, bewildered, and doped as I was, they seemed to have no effect on me—you can't wet a river.

A mermaid came in the door. No scaly tail, surely, but a mermaid is what she looked like. When my eyes refocused I saw that it was a very likely looking and adequately mammalian young woman in singlet and shorts, swimming along head first in a way that made clear that free fall was no novelty to her. She glanced at me without smiling, placed herself against the other cider press, and took hold of the hand grips—she did not bother with safety belts. The music hit the rolling finale and I felt myself grow very heavy.

Two gravities is not bad, not when you are floating in a liquid bed. The skin over the top of the cider press pushed up around me, supporting me inch by inch; I simply felt heavy and found it hard to breathe. You hear these stories about pilots torching at ten gravities and ruining themselves and I have no doubt that they are true—but two gravities, taken in the cider press, simply makes one feel languid, unable to move.

It was some time before I realized that the horn in the ceiling was speaking to me. "Lorenzo! How are you doing, shipmate?"

"All right." The effort made me gasp. "How long do we have to put up with this?"

"About two days."

I must have moaned, for Dak laughed at me. "Quit belly-aching, chum! My first trip to Mars took thirty-seven weeks, every minute of it free fall in an elliptical orbit. You're taking the luxury route, at a mere double gee for a couple of days —with a one-gee rest at turnover, I might add. We ought to charge you for it."

I started to tell him what I thought of his humor in scathing green-room idiom, then recalled that there was a lady present. My father had taught me that a woman will forgive any action, up to and including assault with violence, but is easily insulted by language; the lovelier half of our race is symbol-oriented—very strange, in view of their extreme practicality. In any case, I have never let a taboo word pass my lips when it might offend the ears of a lady since the time I last received the back of my father's hard hand full on my mouth . . . Father could have given Professor Pavlov pointers in reflex conditioning.

But Dak was speaking again. "Penny! You there, honey chile?"

"Yes, Captain," the young woman with me answered.

"Okay, start him on his homework. I'll be down when I have this firetrap settled in its groove."

"Very well, Captain." She turned her head toward me and said in a soft, husky, contralto voice, "Dr. Capek wants you simply to relax and look at movies for several hours. I am here to answer questions as necessary."

I sighed. "Thank goodness someone is at last going to answer questions!"

She did not answer, but raised an arm with some difficulty and passed it over a switch. The lights in the compartment died out and a sound and stereo image built up in front of my eyes. I recognized the central figure—just as any of the billions of citizens of the Empire would have recognized him —and I realized at last how thoroughly and mercilessly Dak Broadbent had tricked me.

It was Bonforte.

The Bonforte, I mean—the Right Honorable John Joseph Bonforte, former Supreme Minister, leader of the loyal opposition, and head of the Expansionist coalition—the most loved (and the most hated!) man in the entire Solar System.

My astonished mind made a standing broad jump and arrived at what seemed a logical certainty. Bonforte had lived through at least three assassination attempts—or so the news reports would have us believe. At least two of his escapes had seemed almost miraculous. Suppose they were not miraculous? Suppose they had all been successful—but dear old Uncle Joe Bonforte had always been somewhere else at the time?

You could use up a lot of actors that way.

3

I had never meddled in politics. My father had warned against it. "Stay out of it, Larry," he had told me solemnly. "The publicity you get that way is bad publicity. The peasants don't like it." I had never voted—not even after the amendment of '98 made it easy for the floating population (which includes, of course, most members of the profession) to exercise franchise.

However, insofar as I had political leanings of any sort, they certainly did not lean toward Bonforte. I considered him a dangerous man and very possibly a traitor to the human race. The idea of standing up and getting killed in his place was—how shall I put it?—distasteful to me.

But—*what* a role!

I had once played the lead in *L'Aiglon* and I had played Caesar in the only two plays about him worthy of the name. But to play such a role *in life*—well, it is enough to make one understand how a man could go to the guillotine in another man's place—just for the chance to play, even for a few moments, the ultimately exacting role, in order to create the supreme, the perfect, work of art.

I wondered who my colleagues had been who had been unable to resist that temptation on those earlier occasions. They had been artists, that was certain—though their very anonymity was the only tribute to the success of their characterizations. I tried to remember just when the earlier attempts on Bonforte's life had taken place and which colleagues who might have been capable of the role had died or dropped out of sight at those times. But it was useless. Not only was I not too sure of the details of current political history but also actors simply fade out of view with depressing frequency; it is a chancy profession even for the best of us.

I found that I had been studying closely the characterization.

I realized I could play it. Hell, I could play it with one foot in a bucket and a smell of smoke backstage. To begin with, there was no problem of physique; Bonforte and I could have swapped clothes without a wrinkle. These childish conspirators who had shanghaied me had vastly overrated the importance of physical resemblance, since it means nothing if not backed up by art—and need not be at all close

32

if the actor is competent. But I admit that it does help and their silly game with the computer machine had resulted (quite by accident!) in selecting a true artist, as well as one who was in measurements and bony structure the twin of the politician. His profile was much like mine; even his hands were long, narrow, and aristocratic like mine—and hands are harder than faces.

That limp, supposedly the result of one of the attempts on his life—nothing to it! After watching him for a few minutes I knew that I could get up from that bed (at one gravity, that is) and walk in precisely the same way and never have to think about it. The way he had of scratching his collarbone and then brushing his chin, the almost imperceptible tic which preceded each of his sentences—such things were no trouble; they soaked into my subconscious like water into sand.

To be sure, he was fifteen or twenty years older than I was, but it is easier to play a role older than oneself than one younger. In any case, age to an actor is simply a matter of inner attitude; it has nothing to do with the steady march of catabolism.

I could have played him on boards, or read a speech in his place, within twenty minutes. But this part, as I understood it, would be more than such an interpretation; Dak had hinted that I would have to convince people who knew him well, perhaps in intimate circumstances. This is surpassingly more difficult. Does he take sugar in his coffee? If so, how much? Which hand does he use to strike a cigarette and with what gesture? I got the answer to that one and planted it deep in my mind even as I phrased the question; the simulacrum in front of me struck a cigarette in a fashion that convinced me that he had used matches and the old-fashioned sort of gasper for years before he had gone along with the march of so-called progress.

Worst of all, a man is not a single complexity; he is a *different* complexity to every person who knows him—which means that, to be successful, an impersonation must change for each "audience"—for each acquaintance of the man being impersonated. This is not merely difficult; it is statistically impossible. Such little things could trip one up. What shared experiences does your principal have with acquaintance John Jones? With a hundred, or a thousand, John Joneses? How could an impersonator possibly know?

Acting *per se*, like all art, is a process of abstracting, of retaining only significant detail. But in impersonation *any* detail can be significant. In time, something as silly as not crunching celery could let the cat out of the bag.

Then I recalled with glum conviction that my performance

probably need be convincing only long enough for a marksman to draw a bead on me.

But I was still studying the man I was to replace (what else could I do?) when the door opened and I heard Dak in his proper person call out, "Anybody home?" The lights came on, the three-dimensional vision faded, and I felt as if I had been wrenched from a dream. I turned my head; the young woman called Penny was struggling to lift her head from the other hydraulic bed and Dak was standing braced in the doorway.

I looked at him and said wonderingly, "How do you manage to stand up?" Part of my mind, the professional part that works independently, was noting how he stood and filing it in a new drawer marked: "How a Man Stands under Two Gravities."

He grinned at me. "Nothing to it. I wear arch supports."

"Hmmmph!"

"You can stand up, if you want to. Ordinarily we discourage passengers from getting out of the boost tanks when we are torching at anything over one and a half gees—too much chance that some idiot will fall over his own feet and break a leg. But I once saw a really tough weight-lifter type climb out of the press and walk at five gravities—but he was never good for much afterwards. But two gees is okay—about like carrying another man piggyback." He glanced at the young lady. "Giving him the straight word, Penny?"

"He hasn't asked anything yet."

"So? Lorenzo, I thought you were the lad who wanted all the answers."

I shrugged. "I cannot now see that it matters, since it is evident that I will not live long enough to appreciate them."

"Eh? What soured your milk, old son?"

"Captain Broadbent," I said bitterly, "I am inhibited in expressing myself by the presence of a lady; therefore I cannot adequately discuss your ancestry, personal habits, morals, and destination. Let it stand that I knew what you had tricked me into as soon as I became aware of the identity of the man I am to impersonate. I will content myself with one question only: who is about to attempt to assassinate Bonforte? Even a clay pigeon should be entitled to know who is shooting at him."

For the first time I saw Dak register surprise. Then he laughed so hard that the acceleration seemed to be too much for him; he slid to the deck and braced his back against a bulkhead, still laughing.

"I don't see anything funny about it," I said angrily.

He stopped and wiped his eyes. "Lorrie old son, did you honestly think that I had set you up as a sitting duck?"

"It's obvious." I told him my deductions about the earlier assassination attempts.

He had the sense not to laugh again. "I see. You thought it was a job about like food taster for a Middle Ages king. Well, we'll have to try to straighten you out; I don't suppose it helps your acting to think that you are about to be burned down where you stand. Look, I've been with the Chief for six years. During that time I *know* he has never used a double . . . Nevertheless, I was present on two occasions when attempts were made on his life—one of those times I shot the hatchet man. Penny, you've been with the Chief longer than that. Has he ever used a double before?"

She looked at me coldly. "Never. The very idea that the Chief would let anybody expose himself to danger in his place is—well, I ought to slap your face; that's what I ought to do!"

"Take it easy, Penny," Dak said mildly. "You've both got jobs to do and you are going to have to work with him. Besides, his wrong guess isn't too silly, not from the outside. By the way, Lorenzo, this is Penelope Russell. She is the Chief's personal secretary, which makes her your number-one coach."

"I am honored to meet you, mademoiselle."

"I wish I could say the same!"

"Stow it, Penny, or I'll spank your round fanny—at two gravities. Lorenzo, I concede that doubling for John Joseph Bonforte isn't as safe as riding in a wheel chair—shucks, as we both know, several attempts have been made to close out his life insurance. But that is not what we are afraid of this time. Matter of fact, this time, for political reasons you will presently understand, the laddies we are up against won't dare to try to kill the Chief—or to kill you when you are doubling for the Chief. They are playing rough—as you *know!*—and they would kill me, or even Penny, for the slightest advantage. They would kill you right now, if they could get at you. But when you make this public appearance *as the Chief* you'll be safe; the circumstances will be such that they can't afford to kill."

He studied my face. "Well?"

I shook my head. "I don't follow you."

"No, but you will. It is a complicated matter, involving Martian ways of looking at things. Take it for granted; you'll know all about it before we get there."

I still did not like it. Thus far Dak had told me no outright lies that I knew of—but he could lie effectively by not telling all that he knew, as I had learned the bitter way. I said, "See here, I have no reason to trust you, or to trust this young lady—if you will pardon me, miss. But while I

35

haven't any liking for Mr. Bonforte, he does have the reputation for being painfully, even offensively, honest. When do I get to talk to *him?* As soon as we reach Mars?"

Dak's ugly, cheerful face was suddenly shadowed with sadness. "I'm afraid not. Didn't Penny tell you?"

"Tell me what?"

"Old son, that's why we've got to have a double for the Chief. They've kidnaped him."

My head ached, possibly from the double weight, or perhaps from too many shocks. "Now you know," Dak went on. "You know why Jock Dubois didn't want to trust you with it until after we raised ground. It is the biggest news story since the first landing on the Moon, and we are sitting on it, doing our damnedest to keep it from ever being known. We hope to use you until we can find him and get him back. Matter of fact, you have already started your impersonation. This ship is not really the *Go For Broke;* it is the Chief's private yacht and traveling office, the *Tom Paine.* The *Go For Broke* is riding a parking orbit around Mars, with its transponder giving out the recognition signal of this ship—a fact known only to its captain and comm officer—while the *Tommie* tucks up her skirts and rushes to Earth to pick up a substitute for the Chief. Do you begin to scan it, old son?"

I admit that I did not. "Yes, but—see here, Captain, if Mr. Bonforte's political enemies have kidnaped him, why keep it secret? I should expect you to shout it from the housetops."

"On Earth we would. At New Batavia we would. On Venus we would. But here we are dealing with Mars. Do you know the legend of Kkkahgral the Younger?"

"Eh? I'm afraid I don't."

"You must study it; it will give you insight into what makes a Martian tick. Briefly, this boy Kkkah was to appear at a certain time and place, thousands of years ago, for a very high honor—like being knighted. Through no fault of his own (the way we would look at it) he failed to make it on time. Obviously the only thing to do was to kill him— by Martian standards. But because of his youth and his distinguished record some of the radicals present argued that he should be allowed to go back and start over. But Kkkahgral would have none of it. He insisted on his right to prosecute the case himself, won it, and was executed. Which makes him the very embodiment, the patron saint, of propriety on Mars."

"That's crazy!"

"Is it? We aren't Martians. They are a very old race and they have worked out a system of debts and obligations to cover every possible situation—the greatest formalists conceivable. Compared with them, the ancient Japanese, with their *giri* and *gimu*, were outright anarchists. Martians don't have 'right' and 'wrong'—instead they have propriety and impropriety, squared, cubed, and loaded with gee juice. But where it bears on this problem is that the Chief was about to be adopted into the nest of Kkkahgral the Younger himself. Do you scan me now?"

I still did not. To my mind this Kkkah character was one of the more loathsome items from *Le Grand Guignol.* Broadbent went on, "It's simple enough. The Chief is probably the greatest practical student of Martian customs and psychology. He has been working up to this for years. Comes local noon on Wednesday at Lacus Soli, the ceremony of adoption takes place. If the Chief is there and goes through his paces properly, everything is sweet. If he is not there— and it makes no difference at all why he is not there—his name is mud on Mars, in every nest from pole to pole—and the greatest interplanetary and interracial political coup ever attempted falls flat on its face. Worse than that, it will backfire. My guess is that the very least that will happen is for Mars to withdraw even from its present loose association with the Empire. Much more likely there will be reprisals and human beings will be killed—maybe every human on Mars. Then the extremists in the Humanity Party would have their way and Mars would be brought into the Empire by force— but only after every Martian was dead. And all set off just by Bonforte failing to show up for the adoption ceremony . . . Martians take these things very seriously."

Dak left as suddenly as he had appeared and Penelope Russell turned on the picture projector again. It occurred to me fretfully that I should have asked him what was to keep our enemies from simply killing *me,* if all that was needed to upset the political applecart was to keep Bonforte (in his proper person, or through his double) from attending some barbaric Martian ceremony. But I had forgotten to ask—perhaps I was subconsciously afraid of being answered.

But shortly I was again studying Bonforte, watching his movements and gestures, feeling his expressions, subvocalizing the tones of his voice, while floating in that detached, warm reverie of artistic effort. Already I was "wearing his head."

I was panicked out of it when the images shifted to one in which Bonforte was surrounded by Martians, touched by their pseudo limbs. I had been so deep inside the picture that I could actually feel them myself—and the stink was unbearable. I made a strangled noise and clawed at it. *"Shut it off!"*

The lights came up and the picture disappeared. Miss

Russell was looking at me. "What in the world is the matter with you?"

I tried to get my breath and stop trembling. "Miss Russell —I am very sorry—but please—don't turn that on again. I can't *stand* Martians."

She looked at me as if she could not believe what she saw but despised it anyhow. "I told them," she said slowly and scornfully, "that this ridiculous scheme would not work."

"I am very sorry. I cannot help it."

She did not answer but climbed heavily out of the cider press. She did not walk as easily at two gravities as Dak did, but she managed. She left without another word, closing the door as she went.

She did not return. Instead the door was opened by a man who appeared to be inhabiting a giant kiddie stroller. "Howdy there, young fellow!" he boomed out. He was sixty-ish, a bit too heavy, and bland; I did not have to see his diploma to be aware that this was a "bedside" manner.

"How do you do, sir?"

"Well enough. Better at lower acceleration." He glanced down at the contrivance he was strapped into. "How do you like my corset-on-wheels? Not stylish, perhaps, but it takes some of the strain off my heart. By the way, just to keep the record straight, I'm Dr. Capek, Mr. Bonforte's personal therapist. I know who you are. Now what's this we hear about you and Martians?"

I tried to explain it clearly and unemotionally.

Dr. Capek nodded. "Captain Broadbent should have told me. I would have changed the order of your indoctrination program. The captain is a competent young fellow in his way but his muscles run ahead of his brain on occasion . . . He is so perfectly normal an extrovert that he frightens me. But no harm done. Mr. Smythe, I want your permission to hypnotize you. You have my word as a physician that it will be used only to help you in this matter and that I will in no wise tamper with your personal integration." He pulled out an old-fashioned pocket watch of the sort that is almost a badge of his profession and took my pulse.

I answered, "You have my permission readily, sir—but it won't do any good. I can't go under." I had learned hypnotic techniques myself during the time I was showing my mentalist act, but my teachers had never had any luck hypnotizing me. A touch of hypnotism is very useful to such an act, especially if the local police aren't too fussy about the laws the medical association has hampered us with.

"So? Well, we'll just have to do the best we can, then. Suppose you relax, get comfortable, and we'll talk about your problem." He still kept the watch in his hand, fiddling

38

with it and twisting the chain, after he had stopped taking my pulse. I started to mention it, since it was catching the reading light just over my head, but decided that it was probably a nervous habit of which he was not aware and really too trivial a matter to call to the attention of a stranger.

"I'm relaxed," I assured him. "Ask me anything you wish. Or free association, if you prefer."

"Just let yourself float," he said softly. "Two gravities makes you feel heavy, doesn't it? I usually just sleep through it myself. It pulls the blood out of the brain, makes one sleepy. They are beginning to boost the drive again. We'll all have to sleep . . . We'll be heavy . . . We'll have to sleep . . ."

I started to tell him that he had better put his watch away—or it would spin right out of his hand. Instead I fell asleep.

When I woke up, the other acceleration bunk was occupied by Dr. Capek. "Howdy, bub," he greeted me. "I got tired of that confounded perambulator and decided to stretch out here and distribute the strain."

"Uh, are we back on two gravities again?"

"Eh? Oh yes! We're on two gravities."

"I'm sorry I blacked out. How long was I asleep?"

"Oh, not very long. How do you feel?"

"Fine. Wonderfully rested, in fact."

"It frequently has that effect. Heavy boost, I mean. Feel like seeing some more pictures?"

"Why, certainly, if you say so, Doctor."

"Okay." He reached up and again the room went dark.

I was braced for the notion that he was going to show me more pictures of Martians; I made up my mind not to panic. After all, I had found it necessary on many occasions to pretend that they were not present; surely motion pictures of them should not affect me—I had simply been surprised earlier.

They were indeed stereos of Martians, both with and without Mr. Bonforte. I found it possible to study them with detached mind, without terror or disgust.

Suddenly I realized that I was *enjoying* looking at them! I let out some exclamation and Capek stopped the film. "Trouble?"

"Doctor—you hypnotized me!"

"You told me to."

"But I can't be hypnotized."

"Sorry to hear it."

"Uh—so you managed it. I'm not too dense to see that."

I added, "Suppose we try those pictures again. I can't really believe it."

He switched them on and I watched and wondered. Martians were not disgusting, if one looked at them without prejudice; they weren't even ugly. In fact, they possessed the same quaint grace as a Chinese pagoda. True, they were not human in form, but neither is a bird of paradise—and birds of paradise are the loveliest things alive.

I began to realize, too, that their pseudo limbs could be very expressive; their awkward gestures showed some of the bumbling friendliness of puppies. I knew now that I had looked at Martians all my life through the dark glasses of hate and fear.

Of course, I mused, their stench would still take getting used to, but—and then I suddenly realized that I was smelling them, the unmistakable odor—and I didn't mind it a bit! In fact, I liked it. "Doctor!" I said urgently. "This machine has a 'smellie' attachment—doesn't it?"

"Eh? I believe not. No, I'm sure it hasn't—too much parasitic weight for a yacht."

"But it must. I can smell them very plainly."

"Oh, yes." He looked slightly shamefaced. "Bub, I did one thing to you that I hope will cause you no inconvenience."

"Sir?"

"While we were digging around inside your skull it became evident that a lot of your neurotic orientation about Martians was triggered by their body odor. I didn't have time to do a deep job so I had to offset it. I asked Penny— that's the youngster who was in here before—for a loan of some of the perfume she uses. I'm afraid that from here on out, bub, Martians are going to smell like a Parisian house of joy to you. If I had had time I would have used some homelier pleasant odor, like ripe strawberries or hot cakes and syrup. But I had to improvise."

I sniffed. Yes, it did smell like a heavy and expensive perfume—and yet, damn it, it was unmistakably the reek of Martians. "I like it."

"You can't help liking it."

"But you must have spilled the whole bottle in here. The place is drenched with it."

"Huh? Not at all. I merely waved the stopper under your nose a half hour ago, then gave the bottle back to Penny and she went away with it." He sniffed. "The odor is gone now. 'Jungle Lust,' it said on the bottle. Seemed to have a lot of musk in it. I accused Penny of trying to make the crew space-happy and she just laughed at me." He reached up and switched off the stereopix. "We've had enough of those for now. I want to get you onto something more useful."

When the pictures faded out, the fragrance faded with them, just as it does with smellie equipment. I was forced to admit to myself that it as all in the head. But, as an actor, I was intellectually aware of that truth anyhow.

When Penny came back in a few minutes later, she had a fragrance exactly like a Martian.

I loved it.

4

My education continued in that room. (Mr. Bonforte's guest room, it was) until turnover. I had no sleep, other than under hypnosis, and did not seem to need any. Either Doc Capek or Penny stuck with me and helped me the whole time. Fortunately my man was as thoroughly photographed and recorded as perhaps any man in history and I had, as well, the close co-operation of his intimates. There was endless material; the problem was to see how much I could assimilate, both awake and under hypnosis.

I don't know at what point I quit disliking Bonforte. Capek assured me—and I believe him—that he did not implant a hypnotic suggestion on this point; I had not asked for it and I am quite certain that Capek was meticulous about the ethical responsibilities of a physician and hypnotherapist. But I suppose that it was an inevitable concomitant of the role—I rather think I would learn to like Jack the Ripper if I studied for the part. Look at it this way: to learn a role truly, you must for a time become that chararter. And a man either likes himself, or he commits suicide, one way or another.

"To understand all is to forgive all"—and I was beginning to understand Bonforte.

At turnover we got that one-gravity rest that Dak had promised. We never were in free fall, not for an instant; instead of putting out the torch, which I gather they hate to do while under way, the ship described what Dak called a 180-degree skew turn. It leaves the ship on boost the whole time and is done rather quickly, but it has an oddly disturbing effect on the sense of balance. The effect has a name something like Coriolanus. Coriolis?

All I know about spaceships is that the ones that operate

41

from the surface of a planet are true rockets but the *voyageurs* call them "teakettles" because of the steam jet of water or hydrogen they boost with. They aren't considered real atomic-power ships even though the jet is heated by an atomic pile. The long-jump ships such as the *Tom Paine*, torchships that is, are (so they tell me) the real thing, making use of E equals MC squared, or is it M equals EC squared? You know—the thing Einstein invented.

Dak did his best to explain it all to me, and no doubt it is very interesting to those who care for such things. But I can't imagine why a gentleman should bother with such. It seems to me that every time those scientific laddies get busy with their slide rules life becomes more complicated. What was wrong with things the way they were?

During the two hours we were on one gravity I was moved up to Bonforte's cabin. I started wearing his clothes and his face and everyone was careful to call me "Mr. Bonforte" or "Chief" or (in the case of Dr. Capek) "Joseph," the idea being, of course, to help me build the part.

Everyone but Penny, that is . . . She simply would not call me "Mr. Bonforte." She did her best to help but she could not bring herself to that. It was clear as scripture that she was a secretary who silently and hopelessly loved her boss, and she resented me with a deep, illogical, but natural bitterness. It made it hard for both of us, especially as I was finding her most attractive. No man can do his best work with a woman constantly around him who despises him. But I could not dislike her in return; I felt deeply sorry for her—even though I was decidedly irked.

We were on a tryout-in-the-sticks basis now, as not everyone in the *Tom Paine* knew that I was not Bonforte. I did not know exactly which ones knew of the substitution, but I was allowed to relax and ask questions only in the presence of Dak, Penny, and Dr. Capek. I was fairly sure that Bonforte's chief clerk, Mr. Washington, knew but never let on; he was a spare, elderly mulatto with the tight-lipped mask of a saint. There were two others who certainly knew, but they were not in the *Tom Paine;* they were standing by and covering up from the *Go For Broke,* handling press releases and routine dispatches—Bill Corpsman, who was Bonforte's front man with the news services, and Roger Clifton. I don't know quite how to describe Clifton's job. Political deputy? He had been Minister without Portfolio, you may remember, when Bonforte was Supreme Minister, but that says nothing. Let's put it symbolically: Bonforte handed out policy and Clifton handed out patronage.

This small group had to know; if any others knew it was not considered necessary to tell me. To be sure, the other members of Bonforte's staff and all the crew of the *Tom Paine* knew that something odd was going on; they did not necessarily know what it was. A good many people had seen me enter the ship—but as "Benny Grey." By the time they saw me again I was already "Bonforte."

Someone had had the foresight to obtain real make-up equipment, but I used almost none. At close range make-up can be seen; even Silicoflesh cannot be given the exact texture of skin. I contented myself with darkening my natural complexion a couple of shades with Semiperm and wearing his face, from inside. I did have to sacrifice quite a lot of hair and Dr. Capek inhibited the roots. I did not mind; an actor can always wear hair-pieces—and I was sure that this job was certain to pay me a fee that would let me retire for life, if I wished.

On the other hand, I was sometimes queasily aware that "life" might not be too long—there are those old saws about the man who knew too much and the one about dead men and tales. But truthfully I was beginning to trust these people. They were all darn nice people—which told me as much about Bonforte as I had learned by listening to his speeches and seeing his pix. A political figure is not a single man, so I was learning, but a compatible team. If Bonforte himself had not been a decent sort he would not have had these people around him.

The Martian language gave me my greatest worry. Like most actors, I had picked up enough Martian, Venerian, Outer Jovian, etc., to be able to fake in front of a camera or on stage. But those rolled or fluttered consonants are very difficult. Human vocal cords are not as versatile as a Martian's tympanus, I believe, and, in any case, the semi-phonetic spelling out of those sounds in Roman letters, for example "kkk" or "jjj" or "rrr," have no more to do with the true sounds than the *g* in "Gnu" has to do with the inhaled click with which a Bantu pronounces "Gnu." "Jjj," for instance, closely resembles a Bronx cheer.

Fortunately Bonforte had no great talent for other languages—and I am a professional; my ears really hear, I can imitate any sound, from a buzz saw striking a nail in a chunk of firewood to a setting hen disturbed on her nest. It was necessary only to acquire Martian as poorly as Bonforte spoke it. He had worked hard to overcome his lack of talent, and every word and phrase of Martian that he knew had been sight-sound recorded so that he could study his mistakes.

So I studied his mistakes, with the projector moved into his office and Penny at my elbow to sort out the spools for me and answer questions.

Human languages fall into four groups: inflecting ones as in Anglo-American, positional as in Chinese, agglutinative as in Old Turkish, polysynthetic (sentence units) as in Eskimo—to which, of course, we now add alien structures as wildly odd and as nearly impossible for the human brain as non-repetitive or emergent Venerian. Luckily Martian is analogous to human speech forms. Basic Martian, the trade language, is positional and involves only simple concrete ideas—like the greeting: "I see you." High Martian is polysynthetic and very stylized, with an expression for every nuance of their complex system of rewards and punishments, obligations and debts. It had been almost too much for Bonforte; Penny told me that he could read those arrays of dots they use for writing quite easily but of the spoken form of High Martian he could say only a few hundred sentences.

Brother, how I studied those few he had mastered!

The strain on Penny was even greater than it was on me. Both she and Dak spoke some Martian but the chore of coaching me fell on her as Dak had to spend most of his time in the control room; Jock's death had left him shorthanded. We dropped from two gravities to one for the last few million miles of the approach, during which time he never came below at all. I spent it learning the ritual I would have to know for the adoption ceremony, with Penny's help.

I had just completed running through the speech in which I was to accept membership in the Kkkah nest—a speech not unlike that, in spirit, with which an orthodox Jewish boy assumes the responsibilities of manhood, but as fixed, as invariable, as Hamlet's soliloquy. I had read it, complete with Bonforte's mispronunciations and facial tic; I finished and asked, "How was that?"

"That was quite good," she answered seriously.

"Thanks, Curly Top." It was a phrase I had lifted from the language-practice spools in Bonforte's files; it was what Bonforte called her when he was feeling mellow—and it was perfectly in character.

"Don't you dare call me that!"

I looked at her in honest amazement and answered, still in character, "Why, Penny my child!"

"Don't you call me *that*, either! You *fake!* You *phony!* You—*actor!*" She jumped up, ran as far as she could—which was only to the door—and stood there, faced away from me, her face buried in her hands and her shoulders shaking with sobs.

I made a tremendous effort and lifted myself out of the

character—pulled in my belly, let my own face come up, answered in my own voice. "Miss Russell!"

She stopped crying, whirled around, looked at me, and her jaw dropped. I added, still in my normal self, "Come back here and sit down."

I thought she was going to refuse, then she seemed to think better of it, came slowly back and sat down, her hands in her lap but with her face that of a little girl who is "saving up more spit."

I let her sit for a moment, then said quietly, "Yes, Miss Russell, I am an actor. Is that a reason for you to insult me?"

She simply looked stubborn.

"As an actor, I am here to an actor's job. You know why. You know, too, that I was tricked into taking it—it is not a job I would have accepted with my eyes open, even in my wildest moments. I hate having to do it considerably more than you hate having me do it—for despite Captain Broadbent's cheerful assurances I am not at all sure that I will come out of it with my skin intact—and I'm awfully fond of my skin; it's the only one I have. I believe, too, that I know why you find it hard to accept me. But is that any reason for you to make my job harder than it has to be?"

She mumbled. I said sharply, "Speak up!"

"It's dishonest! It's *indecent!*"

I sighed. "It certainly is. More than that, it is impossible —without the wholehearted support of the other members of the cast. So let's call Captain Broadbent down here and tell him. Let's call it off."

She jerked her face up and said, "Oh no! We can't do that."

"Why can't we? A far better thing to drop it now than to present it and have it flop. I can't give a performance under these conditions. Let's admit it."

"But—but—we've *got* to! It's necessary."

"Why is it necessary, Miss Russell? Political reasons? I have not the slightest interest in politics—and I doubt if you have any really deep interest. So why must we do it?"

"Because—because *he*——" She stopped, unable to go on, strangled by sobs.

I got up, went over, and put a hand on her shoulder. "I know. Because if we don't, something that . *he* has spent years building up will fall to pieces. Because he can't do it himself and his friends are trying to cover up and do it for him. Because his friends are loyal to him. Because *you* are loyal to him. Nevertheless, it hurts you to see someone else in the place that is rightfully his. Besides that, you are half out of your mind with grief and worry about him. Aren't you?"

"Yes." I could barely hear it.

I took hold of her chin and tilted her face up. "I know why you find it so hard to have me here, in his place. You love him. But I'm doing the best job for him I know how. *Confound it, woman! Do you have to make my job six times harder by treating me like dirt?*"

She looked shocked. For a moment I thought she was going to slap me. Then she said brokenly, "I am sorry. I am very sorry. I won't let it happen again."

I let go her chin and said briskly, "Then let's get back to work."

She did not move. "Can you forgive me?"

"Huh? There's nothing to forgive, Penny. You were acting up because you love him and you were worried. Now let's get to work. I've got to be letter-perfect—and it's only hours away." I dropped at once back into the role.

She picked up a spool and started the projector again. I watched him through it once, then did the acceptance speech with the sound cut out but stereo on, matching my voice—*his* voice, I mean—to the moving image. She watched me, looking from the image back to my face with a dazed look on her own. We finished and I switched it off myself. "How was that?"

"That was perfect!"

I smiled his smile. "Thanks, Curly Top."

"Not at all—'Mr. Bonforte.'"

Two hours later we made rendezvous with the *Go For Broke*.

Dak brought Roger Clifton and Bill Corpsman to my cabin as soon as the *Go For Broke* had transferred them. I knew them from pictures. I stood up and said, "Hello, Rog. Glad to see you, Bill." My voice was warm but casual; on the level at which these people operated, a hasty trip to Earth and back was simply a few days' separation and nothing more. I limped over and offered my hand. The ship was at the moment under low boost as it adjusted to a much tighter orbit than the *Go For Broke* had been riding in.

Clifton threw me a quick glance, then played up. He took his cigar out of his mouth, shook hands, and said quietly, "Glad to see you back, Chief." He was a small man, bald-headed and middle-aged, and looked like a lawyer and a good poker player.

"Anything special while I was away?"

"No. Just routine. I gave Penny the file."

"Good." I turned to Bill Corpsman, again offered my hand. He did not take it. Instead he put his fists on his hips,

46

looked up at me, and whistled. "Amazing! I really do believe we stand a chance of getting away with it." He looked me up and down, then said, "Turn around, Smythe. Move around. I want to see you walk."

I found that I was actually feeling the annoyance that Bonforte would have felt at such uncalled-for impertinence, and, of course, it showed in my face. Dak touched Corpsman's sleeve and said quickly, "Knock it off, Bill. You remember what we agreed?"

"Chicken tracks!" Corpsman answered. "This room is soundproof. I just want to make sure he is up to it. Smythe, how's your Martian? Can you spiel it?"

I answered with a single squeaking polysyllabic in High Martian, a sentence meaning roughly, "Proper conduct demands that one of us leave!"—but it means far more than that, as it is a challenge which usually ends in someone's nest being notified of a demise.

I don't think Corpsman understood it, for he grinned and answered, "I've got to hand it to you, Smythe. That's good."

But Dak understood it. He took Corpsman by the arm and said, "Bill, I told you to knock it off. You're in my ship and that's an order. We play it straight from here on—every second."

Clifton added, "Pay attention to him, Bill. You know we agreed that was the way to do it. Otherwise somebody might slip."

Corpsman glanced at him, then shrugged. "All right, all right. I was just checking up—after all, this was my idea." He gave me a one-sided smile and said, "Howdy, Mister Bonforte. Glad to see you back."

There was a shade too much emphasis on "Mister" but I answered, "Good to be back, Bill. Anything special I need to know before we go down?"

"I guess not. Press conference at Goddard City after the ceremonies." I could see him watching me to see how I would take it.

I nodded. "Very well."

Dak said hastily, "Say, Rog, how about that? Is it necessary? Did you authorize it?"

"I was going to add," Corpsman went on, turning to Clifton, "before the Skipper here got the jitters, that I can take it myself and tell the boys that the Chief has dry laryngitis from the ceremonies—or we can limit it to written questions submitted ahead of time and I'll get the answers written out for him while the ceremonies are going on. Seeing that he looks and sounds so good close up, I would say

47

to risk it. How about it, Mister—'Bonforte'? Think you can swing it?"

"I see no problem involved in it, Bill." I was thinking that if I managed to get by the Martians without a slip I would undertake to ad-lib double talk to a bunch of human reporters as long as they wanted to listen. I had good command of Bonforte's speaking style by now and at least a rough notion of his policies and attitudes—and I need not be specific.

But Clifton looked worried. Before he could speak the ship's horn brayed out, "Captain is requested to come to the control room. Minus four minutes."

Dak said quickly, "You all will have to settle it. I've got to put this sled in its slot—I've got nobody up there but young Epstein." He dashed for the door.

Corpsman called out, "Hey, Skip! I wanted to tell you——" He was out the door and following Dak without waiting to say good-by.

Roger Clifton closed the door Corpsman had left open, came back, and said slowly, "Do you want to risk this press conference?"

"That is up to you. I want to do the job."

"Mmm . . . Then I'm inclined to risk it—if we use the written-questions method. But I'll check Bill's answers myself before you have to give them."

"Very well." I added, "If you can find a way to let me have them ten minutes or so ahead of time, there shouldn't be any difficulty. I'm a very quick study."

He inspected me. "I quite believe it—Chief. All right, I'll have Penny slip the answers to you right after the ceremonies. Then you can excuse yourself to go to the men's room and just stay there until you are sure of them."

"That should work."

"I think so. Uh, I must say I feel considerably better now that I've seen you. Is there anything I can do for you?"

"I think not, Rog. Yes, there is, too. Any word about—*him?*"

"Eh? Well, yes and no. He's still in Goddard City; we're sure of that. He hasn't been taken off Mars, or even out in the country. We blocked them on that, if that was their intention."

"Eh? Goddard City is not a big place, is it? Not more than a hundred thousand? What's the hitch?"

"The hitch is that we don't dare admit that you—I mean that *he*—is missing. Once we have this adoption thing wrapped up, we can put you out of sight, then announce the kidnaping as if it had just taken place—and make them take the city apart rivet by rivet. The city authorities are all

48

Humanity Party appointees, but they will have to co-operate —after the ceremony. It will be the most wholehearted co-operation you ever saw, for they will be deadly anxious to produce him before the whole Kkkahgral nest swarms over them and tears the city down around their ears."

"Oh. I'm still learning about Martian psychology and customs."

"Aren't we all!"

"Rog? Mmm . . . What leads you to think that he is still alive? Wouldn't their purpose be better served—and with less risk—just by killing him?" I was thinking queasily how simple it had turned out to be to get rid of a body, if a man was ruthless enough.

"I see what you mean. But that, too, is tied up with Martian notions about 'propriety.' " (He used the Martian word.) "Death is the one acceptable excuse for not carrying out an obligation. If he were simply killed, they would adopt him into the nest after his death—and then the whole nest and probably every nest on Mars would set out to avenge him. They would not mind in the least if the whole human race were to die or be killed—but to kill this one human being to keep him from being adopted, that's another kettle of fish entirely. Matter of obligation and propriety— in some ways a Martian's response to a situation is so automatic as to remind one of instinct. It is not, of course, since they are incredibly intelligent. But they do the damnedest things." He frowned and added, "Sometimes I wish I had never left Sussex."

The warning hooter broke up the discussion by forcing us to hurry to our bunks. Dak had cut it fine on purpose; the shuttle rocket from Goddard City was waiting for us when we settled into free fall. All five of us went down, which just filled the passenger couches—again a matter of planning, for the Resident Commissioner had expressed the intention of coming up to meet me and had been dissuaded only by Dak's message to him that our party would require all the space.

I tried to get a better look at the Martian surface as we went down, as I had had only one glimpse of it, from the control room of the *Tom Paine*—since I was supposed to have been there many times I could not show the normal curiosity of a tourist. I did not get much of a look; the shuttle pilot did not turn us so that we could see until he leveled off for his glide approach and I was busy then putting on my oxygen mask.

That pesky Mars-type mask almost finished us; I had never had a chance to practice with it—Dak did not think of it and I had not realized it would be a problem; I had

49

worn both space suit and aqua lung on other occasions and I thought this would be about the same. It was not. The model Bonforte favored was a mouth-free type, a Mitsubushi "Sweet Winds" which pressurizes directly at the nostrils—a nose clamp, nostril plugs, tubes up each nostril which then run back under each ear to the supercharger on the back of your neck. I concede that it is a fine device, once you get used to it, since you can talk, eat, drink, etc., while wearing it. But I would rather have a dentist put both hands in my mouth.

The real difficulty is that you have to exercise conscious control on the muscles that close the back of your mouth, or you hiss like a teakettle, since the durn thing operates on a pressure difference. Fortunately the pilot equalized to Mars-surface pressure once we all had our masks on, which gave me twenty minutes or so to get used to it. But for a few moments I thought the jig was up, just over a silly piece of gadgetry. But I reminded myself that I had worn the thing hundreds of times before and that I was as used to it as I was to my toothbrush. Presently I believed it.

Dak had been able to avoid having the Resident Commissioner chit-chat with me for an hour on the way down but it had not been possible to miss him entirely; he met the shuttle at the sky field. The close timing did keep me from having to cope with other humans, since I had to go at once into the Martian city. It made sense, but it seemed strange that I would be safer among Martians than among my own kind.

It seemed even stranger to be on Mars.

5

Mr. Commissioner Boothroyd was a Humanity Party appointee, of course, as were all of his staff except for civil service technical employees. But Dak had told me that it was at least sixty-forty that Boothroyd had not had a finger in the plot; Dak considered him honest but stupid. For that matter, neither Dak nor Rog Clifton believed that Supreme Minister Quiroga was in it; they attributed the thing to the clandestine terrorist group inside the Humanity Party who called themselves the "Actionists"—and they attributed *them* to some highly respectable big-money boys who stood to profit heavily.

50

Myself, I would not have known an Actionist from an auctioneer.

But the minute we landed something popped up that made me wonder whether friend Boothroyd was as honest and stupid as Dak thought he was. It was a minor thing but one of those little things that can punch holes in an impersonation. Since I was a Very Important Visitor the Commissioner met me; since I held no public office other than membership in the Grand Assembly and was traveling privately no official honors were offered. He was alone save for his aide—and a little girl about fifteen.

I knew him from photographs and I knew quite a bit about him; Rog and Penny had briefed me carefully. I shook hands, asked about his sinusitis, thanked him for the pleasant time I had had on my last visit, and spoke with his aide in that warm man-to-man fashion that Bonforte was so good at. Then I turned to the young lady. I knew Boothroyd had children and that one of them was about this age and sex; I did not know—perhaps Rog and Penny did not know—whether or not I had ever met her.

Boothroyd himself saved me. "You haven't met my daughter Deirdre, I believe. She insisted on coming along."

Nothing in the pictures I had studied had shown Bonforte dealing with young girls—so I simply had to *be* Bonforte—a widower in his middle fifties who had no children of his own, no nieces, and probably little experience with teen-age girls—but with lots of experience in meeting strangers of every sort. So I treated her as if she were twice her real age; I did not quite kiss her hand. She blushed and looked pleased.

Boothroyd looked indulgent and said, "Well, ask him, my dear. You may not have another chance."

She blushed deeper and said, "Sir, could I have your autograph? The girls in my school collect them. I have Mr. Quiroga's . . . I ought to have yours." She produced a little book which she had been holding behind her.

I felt like a copter driver asked for his license—which is home in his other pants. I had studied hard but I had not expected to have to forge Bonforte's signature. Damn it, you can't do *everything* in two and a half days!

But it was simply impossible for Bonforte to refuse such a request—and I was Bonforte. I smiled jovially and said, "You have Mr. Quiroga's already?"

"Yes, sir."

"Just his autograph?"

"Yes. Er, he put 'Best Wishes' on it."

I winked at Boothroyd. "Just 'Best Wishes,' eh? To young ladies I never make it less than 'Love.' Tell you what I'm going to do——" I took the little book from her, glanced through the pages.

"Chief," Dak said urgently, "we are short on minutes."

"Compose yourself," I said without looking up. "The entire Martian nation can wait, if necessary, on a young lady." I handed the book to Penny. "Will you note the size of this book? And then remind me to send a photograph suitable for pasting in it—and properly autographed, of course."

"Yes, Mr. Bonforte."

"Will that suit you, Miss Deirdre?"

"Gee!"

"Good. Thanks for asking me. We can leave now, Captain. Mr. Commissioner, is that our car?"

"Yes, Mr. Bonforte." He shook his head wryly. "I'm afraid you have converted a member of my own family to your Expansionist heresies. Hardly sporting, eh? Sitting ducks, and so forth?"

"That should teach you not to expose her to bad company—eh, Miss Deirdre?" I shook hands again. "Thanks for meeting us, Mr. Commissioner. I am afraid we had better hurry along now."

"Yes, certainly. Pleasure."

"Thanks, Mr. Bonforte!"

"Thank *you*, my dear."

I turned away slowly, so as not to appear jerky or nervous in stereo. There were photographers around, still, news pickup, stereo, and so forth, as well as many reporters. Bill was keeping the reporters away from us; as we turned to go he waved and said, "See you later, Chief," and turned back to talk to one of them. Rog, Dak, and Penny followed me into the car. There was the usual skyfield crowd, not as numerous as at any earthport, but numerous. I was not worried about them as long as Boothroyd accepted the impersonation—though there were certainly some present who *knew* that I was not Bonforte.

But I refused to let those individuals worry me, either. They could cause us no trouble without incriminating themselves.

The car was a Rolls Outlander, pressurized, but I left my oxygen mask on because the others did. I took the right-hand seat, Rog sat beside me, and Penny beside him, while Dak wound his long legs around one of the folding seats. The driver glanced back through the partition and started up.

Rog said quietly, "I was worried there for a moment."

"Nothing to worry about. Now let's all be quiet, please. I want to review my speech."

Actually I wanted to gawk at the Martian scene; I knew

the speech perfectly. The driver took us along the north edge of the field, past many godowns. I read signs for Verwijs Trading Company, Diana Outlines, Ltd., Three Planets, and I. G. Farbenindustrie. There were almost as many Martians as humans in sight. We ground hogs get the impression that Martians are slow as snails—and they are, on our comparatively heavy planet. On their own world they skim along on their bases like a stone sliding over water.

To the right, south of us past the flat field, the Great Canal dipped into the too-close horizon, showing no shore line beyond. Straight ahead of us was the Nest of Kkkah, a fairy city. I was staring at it, my heart lifting at its fragile beauty, when Dak moved suddenly.

We were well past the traffic around the godowns but there was one car ahead, coming toward us; I had seen it without noticing it. But Dak must have been edgily ready for trouble; when the other car was quite close, he suddenly slammed down the partition separating us from the driver, swarmed over the man's neck, and grabbed the wheel. We slewed to the right, barely missing the other car, slewed again to the left and barely stayed on the road. It was a near thing, for we were past the field now and here the highway edged the canal.

I had not been much use to Dak a couple of days earlier in the Eisenhower, but I had been unarmed and not expecting trouble. This day I was still unarmed, not so much as a poisoned fang, but I comported myself a little better. Dak was more than busy trying to drive the car while leaning over from the back seat. The driver, caught off balance at first, now tried to wrestle him away from the wheel.

I lunged forward, got my left arm around the driver's neck, and shoved my right thumb into his ribs. "Move and you've had it!" The voice belonged to the hero-villain in *The Second-Story Gentleman;* the line of dialogue was his too.

My prisoner became very quiet.

Dak said urgently, "Rog, what are they doing?"

Clifton looked back and answered, "They're turning around."

Dak answered, "Okay. Chief, keep your gun on that character while I climb over." He was doing so even as he spoke, an awkward matter in view of his long legs and the crowded car. He settled into the seat and said happily, "I doubt if anything on wheels can catch a Rolls on a straightaway." He jerked on the damper and the big car shot forward. "How am I doing, Rog?"

"They're just turned around."

"All right. What do we do with this item? Dump him out?"

My victim squirmed and said, "I didn't do anything!" I jabbed my thumb harder and he quieted.

"Oh, not a thing," Dak agreed, keeping his eyes on the road. "All you did was try to cause a little crash—just enough to make Mr. Bonforte late for his appointment. If I had not noticed that you were slowing down to make it easy on yourself, you might have got away with it. No guts, eh?" He took a slight curve with the tires screaming and the gyro fighting to keep us upright. "What's the situation, Rog?"

"They've given up."

"So." Dak did not slacken speed; we must have been doing well over three hundred kilometers. "I wonder if they would try to bomb us with one of their own boys aboard? How about it, bub? Would they write you off as expendable?"

"I don't know what you're talking about! You're going to be in trouble over this!"

"Really? The word of four respectable people against your jailbird record? Or aren't you a transportee? Anyhow, Mr. Bonforte prefers to have me drive him—so naturally you were glad to do a favor for Mr. Bonforte." We hit something about as big as a worm cast on that glassy road and my prisoner and I almost went through the roof.

" 'Mr. Bonforte!' " My victim made it a swear word.

Dak was silent for several seconds. At last he said, "I don't think we ought to dump this one, Chief. I think we ought to let you off, then take him to a quiet place. I think he might talk if we urged him."

The driver tried to get away. I tightened the pressure on his neck and jabbed him again with my thumb knuckle. A knuckle may not feel too much like the muzzle of a heater—but who wants to find out? He relaxed and said sullenly, "You don't dare give me the needle."

"Heavens, no!" Dak answered in shocked tones. "That would be illegal. Penny girl, got a bobby pin?"

"Why, certainly, Dak." She sounded puzzled and I was. She did not sound frightened, though, and I certainly was.

"Good. Bub, did you ever have a bobby pin shoved up under your fingernails? They say it will even break a hypnotic command not to talk. Works directly on the subconscious or something. Only trouble is that the patient makes the most unpleasant noises. So we are going to take you out in the dunes where you won't disturb anybody but sand scorpions. After you have talked—now here comes the nice part! After you talk we are going to turn you loose, not do anything, just let you walk back into town. But—

listen carefully now!—if you are real nice and co-operative, you get a prize. We'll let you have your mask for the walk."

Dak stopped talking; for a moment there was no sound but the keening of the thin Martian air past the roof. A human being can walk possibly two hundred yards on Mars without an oxygen mask, if he is in good condition. I believe I read of a case where a man walked almost half a mile before he died. I glanced at the trip meter and saw that we were about twenty-three kilometers from Goddard City.

The prisoner said slowly, "Honest, I don't know anything about it. I was just paid to crash the car."

"We'll try to stimulate your memory." The gates of the Martian city were just ahead of us; Dak started slowing the car. "Here's where you get out, Chief. Rog, better take your gun and relieve the Chief of our guest."

"Right, Dak." Rog moved up by me, jabbed the man in the ribs—again with a bare knuckle. I moved out of the way. Dak braked the car to a halt, stopping right in front of the gates.

"Four minutes to spare," he said happily. "This is a nice car. I wish I owned it. Rog, ease up a touch and give me room."

Clifton did so, Dak chopped the driver expertly on the side of his neck with the edge of his hand; the man went limp. "That will keep him quiet while you get clear. Can't have any unseemly disturbance under the eyes of the nest. Let's check time."

We did so. I was about three and a half minutes ahead of the deadline. "You are to go in exactly on time, you understand? Not ahead, not behind, but on the dot."

"That's right," Clifton and I answered in chorus.

"Thirty seconds to walk up the ramp, maybe. What do you want to do with the three minutes you have left?"

I sighed. "Just get my nerve back."

"Your nerve is all right. You didn't miss a trick back there. Cheer up, old son. Two hours from now you can head for home, with your pay burning holes in your pocket. We're on the last lap."

"I hope so. It's been quite a strain. Uh, Dak?"

"Yes?"

"Come here a second." I got out of the car, motioned him to come with me a short distance away. "What happens if I made a mistake—in there?"

"Eh?" Dak looked surprised, then laughed a little too heartily. "You won't make a mistake. Penny tells me you've got it down Jo-block perfect."

"Yes, but suppose I slip?"

"You won't slip. I know how you feel; I felt the same way on my first solo grounding. But when it started, I was so busy doing it I didn't have time to do it wrong."

Clifton called out, his voice thin in thin air, "Dak! Are you watching the time?"

"Gobs of time. Over a minute."

"Mr. Bonforte!" It was Penny's voice. I turned and went back to the car. She got out and put out her hand. "Good luck, Mr. Bonforte."

"Thanks, Penny."

Rog shook hands and Dak clapped me on the shoulder. "Minus thirty-five seconds. Better start."

I nodded and started up the ramp. It must have been within a second or two of the exact, appointed time when I reached the top, for the mighty gates rolled back as I came to them. I took a deep breath and cursed that damned air mask.

Then I took my stage.

It doesn't make any difference how many times you do it, that first walk on as the curtain goes up on the first night of any run is a breath-catcher and a heart-stopper. Sure, you know your sides. Sure, you've asked the manager to count the house. Sure, you've done it all before. No matter—when you first walk out there and know that all those eyes are on you, waiting for you to speak, waiting for you to do something—maybe even waiting for you to go up on your lines, brother, you feel it. This is why they have prompters.

I looked out and saw my audience and I wanted to run. I had stage fright for the first time in thirty years.

The siblings of the nest were spread out before me as far as I could see. There was an open lane in front of me, with thousands on each side, set close together as asparagus. I knew that the first thing I must do was slow-march down the center of that lane, clear to the far end, to the ramp leading down into the inner nest.

I could not move.

I said to myself, "Look, boy, you're John Joseph Bonforte. You've been here dozens of times before. These people are your friends. You're here because you want to be here—and because they want you here. So march down that aisle. Tum tum te *tum!* 'Here comes the bride!' "

I began to feel like Bonforte again. I was Uncle Joe Bonforte, determined to do this thing perfectly—for the honor and welfare of my own people and my own planet —and for my friends the Martians. I took a deep breath and one step.

That deep breath saved me; it brought me that heavenly

fragrance. Thousands on thousands of Martians packed close together—it smelled to me as if somebody had dropped and broken a whole case of Jungle Lust. The conviction that I smelled it was so strong that I involuntarily glanced back to see if Penny had followed me in. I could feel her handclasp warm in my palm.

I started limping down that aisle, trying to make it about the speed a Martian moves on his own planet. The crowd closed in behind me. Occasionally kids would get away from their elders and skitter out in front of me. By "kids" I mean post-fission Martians, half the mass and not much over half the height of an adult. They are never out of the nest and we are inclined to forget that there can be little Martians. It takes almost five years, after fission, for a Martian to regain his full size, have his brain fully restored, and get all of his memory back. During this transition he is an idiot studying to be a moron. The gene rearrangement and subsequent regeneration incident to conjugation and fission put him out of the running for a long time. One of Bonforte's spools was a lecture on the subject, accompanied by some not very good amateur stereo.

The kids, being cheerful idiots, are exempt from propriety and all that that implies. But they are greatly loved.

Two of the kids, of the same and smallest size and looking just alike to me, skittered out and stopped dead in front of me, just like a foolish puppy in traffic. Either I stopped or I ran them down.

So I stopped. They moved even closer, blocking my way completely, and started sprouting pseudo limbs while chittering at each other. I could not understand them at all. Quickly they were plucking at my clothes and snaking their patty-paws into my sleeve pockets.

The crowd was so tight that I could hardly go around them. I was stretched between two needs. In the first place they were so darn cute that I wanted to see if I didn't have a sweet tucked away somewhere for them—but in a still firster place was the knowledge that the adoption ceremony was timed like a ballet. If I didn't get on down that street, I was going to commit the classic sin against propriety made famous by Kkkahgral the Younger himself.

But the kids were not about to get out of my way. One of them had found my watch.

I sighed and was almost overpowered by the perfume. Then I made a bet with myself. I bet that baby-kissing was a Galactic Universal and that it took precedence even over Martian propriety. I got on one knee, making myself about the height they were, and fondled them for a few moments, patting them and running my hands down their scales.

57

Then I stood up and said carefully, "That is all now. I must go," which used up a large fraction of my stock of Basic Martian.

The kids clung to me but I moved them carefully and gently aside and went on down the double line, hurrying to make up for the time I had lost. No life wand burned a hole in my back. I risked a hope that my violation of propriety had not yet reached the capital offense level. I reached the ramp leading down into the inner nest and started on down.

* * * * * * * * * * * * *

That line of astericks represents the adoption ceremony. Why? Because it is limited to members of the Kkkah nest. It is a family matter.

Put it this way: A Mormon may have very close gentile friends—but does that friendship get a gentile inside the Temple at Salt Lake City? It never has and it never will. Martians visit very freely back and forth between their nests —but a Martian enters the inner nest only of his own family. Even his conjugate-spouses are not thus privileged. I have no more right to tell the details of the adoption ceremony than a lodge brother has to be specific about ritual outside the lodge.

Oh, the rough outlines do not matter, since they are the same for any nest, just as my part was the same for any candidate. My sponsor—Bonforte's oldest Martian friend, Kkkahrrreash—met me at the door and threatened me with a wand. I demanded that he kill me at once were I guilty of any breach. To tell the truth, I did not recognize him, even though I had studied a picture of him. But it had to be him because ritual required it.

Having thus made clear that I stood four-square for Motherhood, the Home, Civic Virtue, and never missing Sunday school, I was permitted to enter. 'Rrreash conducted me around all the stations, I was questioned and I responded. Every word, every gesture, was as stylized as a classical Chinese play, else I would not have stood a chance. Most of the time I did not know what they were saying and half of the time I did not understand my own replies; I simply knew my cues and the responses. It was not made easier by the low light level the Martians prefer; I was groping around like a mole.

I played once with Hawk Mantell, shortly before he died, after he was stone-deaf. There was a trouper! He could not even use a hearing device because the eighth nerve was dead. Part of the time he could cue by lips but that is not always possible. He directed the production himself and he timed it perfectly. I have seen him deliver a line, walk away—then whirl around and snap out a retort to a line that he had never heard, precisely on the timing.

This was like that. I knew my part and I played it. If *they* blew it, that was their lookout.

But it did not help my morale that there were never less than half a dozen wands leveled at me the whole time. I kept telling myself that they wouldn't burn me down for a slip. After all, I was just a poor stupid human being and at the very least they would give me a passing mark for effort. But I didn't believe it.

After what seemed like days—but was not, since the whole ceremony times exactly one ninth of Mars' rotation—after an endless time, we ate. I don't know what and perhaps it is just as well. It did not poison me.

After that the elders made their speeches, I made my acceptance speech in answer, and they gave me my name and my wand. I was a Martian.

I did not know how to use the wand and my name sounded like a leaky faucet, but from that instant on it was my legal name on Mars and I was legally a blood member of the most aristocratic family on the planet—exactly fifty-two hours after a ground hog down on his luck had spent his last half-Imperial buying a drink for a stranger in the bar of Casa Mañana.

I guess this proves that one should never pick up strangers.

I got out as quickly as possible. Dak had made up a speech for me in which I claimed proper necessity for leaving at once and they let me go. I was nervous as a man upstairs in a sorority house because there was no longer ritual to guide me. I mean to say even casual social behavior was still hedged around with airtight and risky custom and I did not know the moves. So I recited my excuse and headed out. 'Rrreash and another elder went with me and I chanced playing with another pair of the kids when we were outside—or maybe the same pair. Once I reached the gates the two elders said good-by in squeaky English and let me go out alone; the gates closed behind me and I reswallowed my heart.

The Rolls was waiting where they had let me out; I hurried down, a door opened, and I was surprised to see that Penny was in it alone. But not displeased. I called out, "Hi, Curly Top! I made it!"

"I knew you would."

I gave a mock sword salute with my wand and said, "Just call me Kkkahjjjerrr"—spraying the front rows with the second syllable.

"Be careful with that thing!" she said nervously.

I slid in beside her on the front seat and asked, "Do you know how to use one of these things?" The reaction was setting in and I felt exhausted but gay; I wanted three quick drinks and a thick steak, then to wait up for the critics' reviews.

"No. But do be careful."

"I think all you have to do is to press it here," which I did, and there was a neat two-inch hole in the windshield and the car wasn't pressurized any longer.

Penny gasped. I said, "Gee, I'm sorry. I'll put it away until Dak can coach me."

She gulped. "It's all right. Just be careful where you point it." She started wheeling the car and I found that Dak was not the only one with a heavy hand on the damper.

Wind was whistling in through the hole I had made. I said, "What's the rush? I need some time to study my lines for the press conference. Did you bring them? And where are the others?" I had forgotten completely the driver we had grabbed; I had not thought about him from the time the gates of the nest opened.

"No. They couldn't come."

"Penny, what's the matter? What's happened?" I was wondering if I could possibly take a press conference without coaching. Perhaps I could tell them a little about the adoption; I wouldn't have to fake that.

"It's Mr. Bonforte—*they've found him.*"

6

I had not noticed until then that she had not once called me "Mr. Bonforte." She could not, of course, for I was no longer he; I was again Lorrie Smythe, that actor chap they had hired to stand in for him.

I sat back and sighed, and let myself relax. "So it's over at last—and we got away with it." I felt a great burden lift off me; I had not known how heavy it was until I put it down. Even my "lame" leg stopped aching. I reached over and patted Penny's hand on the wheel and said in my own voice, "I'm glad it's over. But I'm going to miss having you around, pal. You're a trouper. But even the best run ends and the company breaks up. I hope I'll see you again sometime."

"I hope so too."

"I suppose Dak has arranged some shenanigan to keep me under cover and snake me back into the *Tom Paine?*"

"I don't know." Her voice sounded odd and I gave her a quick glance and saw that she was crying. My heart gave a skip. Penny crying? Over us separating? I could not believe it and yet I wanted to. One might think that, between my handsome features and cultivated manners, women would find me irresistible, but it is a deplorable fact that all too many of them have found me easy to resist. Penny had seemed to find it no effort at all.

"Penny," I said hastily, "why all the tears, hon? You'll wreck this car."

"I can't help it."

"Well—put me in it. What's wrong? You told me they had got him back; you didn't tell me anything else." I had a sudden horrid but logical suspicion. "He was *alive*—wasn't he?"

"Yes—he's alive—but, oh, they've *hurt* him!" She started to sob and I had to grab the wheel.

She straightened up quickly. "Sorry."

"Want me to drive?"

"I'll be all right. Besides, you don't know how—I mean you aren't supposed to know how to drive."

"Huh? Don't be silly. I do know how and it no longer matters that——" I broke off, suddenly realizing that it might still matter. If they had roughed up Bonforte so that it showed, then he could not appear in public in that shape—at least not only fifteen minutes after being adopted into the Kkkah nest. Maybe I would have to take that press conference and depart publicly, while Bonforte would be the one they would sneak aboard. Well, all right—hardly more than a curtain call. "Penny, do Dak and Rog want me to stay in character for a bit? Do I play to the reporters? Or don't I?"

"I don't know. There wasn't time."

We were already approaching the stretch of godowns by the field, and the giant bubble domes of Goddard City were in sight. "Penny, slow this car down and talk sense. I've got to have my cues."

The driver had talked—I neglected to ask whether or not the bobby-pin treatment had been used. He had then been turned loose to walk back but had not been deprived of his mask; the others had barreled back to Goddard City, with Dak at the wheel. I felt lucky to have been left behind; *voyageurs* should not be allowed to drive anything but spaceships.

They went to the address the driver had given them, in Old Town under the original bubble. I gathered that it was

61

the sort of jungle every port has had since the Phoenicians sailed through the shoulder of Africa, a place of released transportees, prostitutes, monkey-pushers, rangees, and other dregs—a neighborhood where policemen travel only in pairs.

The information they had squeezed out of the driver had been correct but a few minutes out of date. The room had housed the prisoner, certainly, for there was a bed in it which seemed to have been occupied continuously for at least a week, a pot of coffee was still hot—and wrapped in a towel on a shelf was an old-fashioned removable denture which Clifton identified as belonging to Bonforte. But Bonforte himself was missing and so were his captors.

They had left there with the intention of carrying out the original plan, that of claiming that the kidnaping had taken place immediately after the adoption and putting pressure on Boothroyd by threatening to appeal to the Nest of Kkkah. But they had found Bonforte, had simply run across him in the street before they left Old Town—a poor old stumble-bum with a week's beard, dirty and dazed. The men had not recognized him, but Penny had known him and made them stop.

She broke into sobs again as she told me this part and we almost ran down a truck train snaking up to one of the loading docks.

A reasonable reconstruction seemed to be that the laddies in the second car—the one that was to crash us—had reported back, whereupon the faceless leaders of our opponents had decided that the kidnaping no longer served their purposes. Despite the arguments I had heard about it, I was surprised that they had not simply killed him; it was not until later that I understood that what they had done was subtler, more suited to their purposes, and much crueler than mere killing.

"Where is he now?" I asked.

"Dak took him to the *voyageurs'* hostel in Dome 3."

"Is that where we are headed?"

"I don't know. Rog just said to go pick you up, then they disappeared in the service door of the hostel. Uh, no, I don't think we dare go there. I don't know what to do."

"Penny, stop the car."

"Huh?"

"Surely this car has a phone. We won't stir another inch until we find out—or figure out—what we should do. But I am certain of one thing: I should stay in character until Dak or Rog decides that I should fade out. Somebody has to talk to the newsmen. Somebody has to make a public departure for the *Tom Paine*. You're sure that Mr. Bonforte can't be spruced up so that he can do it?"

"What? Oh, he couldn't possibly. You didn't *see* him."

62

"So I didn't. I'll take your word for it. All right, Penny, I'm 'Mr. Bonforte' again and you're my secretary. We'd better get with it."

"Yes—Mr. Bonforte."

"Now try to get Captain Broadbent on the phone, will you, please?"

We couldn't find a phone list in the car and she had to go through "Information," but at last she was tuned with the clubhouse of the *voyageurs*. I could hear both sides. "Pilots' Club, Mrs. Kelly speaking."

Penny covered the microphone. "Do I give my name?"

"Play it straight. We've nothing to hide."

"This is Mr. Bonforte's secretary," she said gravely. "Is his pilot there? Captain Broadbent."

"I know him, dearie." There was a shout: "Hey! Any of you smokers see where Dak went?" After a pause she went on, "He's gone to his room. I'm buzzing him."

Shortly Penny said, "Skipper? The Chief wants to talk to you," and handed me the phone.

"This is the Chief, Dak."

"Oh. Where are you—sir?"

"Still in the car. Penny picked me up. Dak, Bill scheduled a press conference, I believe. Where is it?"

He hesitated. "I'm glad you called in, sir. Bill canceled it. There's been a—slight change in the situation."

"So Penny told me. I'm just as well pleased; I'm rather tired. Dak, I've decided not to stay dirtside tonight; my gimp leg has been bothering me and I'm looking forward to a real rest in free fall." I hated free fall but Bonforte did not. "Will you or Rog make my apologies to the Commissioner, and so forth?"

"We'll take care of everything, sir."

"Good. How soon can you arrange a shuttle for me?"

"The *Pixie* is still standing by for you, sir. If you will go to Gate 3, I'll phone and have a field car pick you up."

"Very good. Out."

"Out, sir."

I handed the phone to Penny to put back in its clamp. "Curly Top, I don't know whether that phone frequency is monitored or not—or whether possibly the whole car is bugged. If either is the case, they may have learned two things—where Dak is and through that where *he* is, and second, what I am about to do next. Does that suggest anything to your mind?"

She looked thoughtful, then took out her secretary's notebook, wrote in it: *Let's get rid of the car.*

I nodded, then took the book from her and wrote in it: *How far away is Gate 3?*

63

She answered: *Walking distance.*

Silently we climbed out and left. She had pulled into some executive's parking space outside one of the warehouses when she had parked the car; no doubt in time it would be returned where it belonged—and such minutiae no longer mattered.

We had gone about fifty yards, when I stopped. Something was the matter. Not the day, certainly. It was almost balmy, with the sun burning brightly in clear, purple Martian sky. The traffic, wheel and foot, seemed to pay no attention to us, or at least such attention was for the pretty young woman with me rather than directed at me. Yet I felt uneasy.

"What is it, Chief?"

"Eh? *That* is what it is!"

"Sir?"

"I'm not being the 'Chief.' It isn't in character to go dodging off like this. Back we go, Penny."

She did not argue, but followed me back to the car. This time I climbed into the back seat, sat there looking dignified, and let her chauffeur me to Gate 3.

It was not the gate we had come in. I think Dak had chosen it because it ran less to passengers and more to freight. Penny paid no attention to signs and ran the big Rolls right up to the gate. A terminal policeman tried to stop her; she simply said coldly, "Mr. Bonforte's car. And will you please send word to the Commissioner's office to call for it here?"

He looked baffled, glanced into the rear compartment, seemed to recognize me, saluted, and let us stay. I answered with a friendly wave and he opened the door for me. "The lieutenant is very particular about keeping the space back of the fence clear, Mr. Bonforte," he apologized, "but I guess it's all right."

"You can have the car moved at once," I said. "My secretary and I are leaving. Is my field car here?"

"I'll find out at the gate, sir." He left. It was just the amount of audience I wanted, enough to tie it down solid that "Mr. Bonforte" had arrived by official car and had left for his space yacht. I tucked my life wand under my arm like Napoleon's baton and limped after him, with Penny tagging along. The cop spoke to the gatemaster, then hurried back to us, smiling. "Field car is waiting, sir."

"Thanks indeed." I was congratulating myself on the perfection of the timing.

"Uh . . ." The cop looked flustered and added hurriedly, in a low voice, "I'm an Expansionist, too, sir. Good job you did today." He glanced at the life wand with a touch of awe.

I knew exactly how Bonforte should look in this routine.

"Why, thank you. I hope you have lots of children. We need to work up a solid majority."

He guffawed more than it was worth. "That's a good one! Uh, mind if I repeat it?"

"Not at all." We had moved on and I started through the gate. The gatemaster touched my arm. "Er . . . Your passport, Mr. Bonforte."

I trust I did not let my expression change. "The passports, Penny."

She looked frostily at the official. "Captain Broadbent takes care of all clearances."

He looked at me and looked away. "I suppose it's all right. But I'm supposed to check them and take down the serial numbers."

"Yes, of course. Well, I suppose I must ask Captain Broadbent to run out to the field. Has my shuttle been assigned a take-off time? Perhaps you had better arrange with the tower to 'hold.' "

But Penny appeared to be cattily angry. "Mr. Bonforte, this is ridiculous! We've *never* had this red tape before—certainly not on *Mars*."

The cop said hastily, "Of course it's all right, Hans. After all, this is Mr. Bonforte."

"Sure, but——"

I interrupted with a happy smile. "There's a simpler way out. If you—what is your name, sir?"

"Haslwanter. Hans Haslwanter," he answered reluctantly.

"Mr. Haslwanter, if you will call Mr. Commissioner Boothroyd, I'll speak to him and we can save my pilot a trip out to the field—and save me an hour or more of time."

"Uh—I wouldn't like to do that, sir. I could call the port captain's office?" he suggested hopefully.

"Just get me Mr. Boothroyd's number. *I* will call him." This time I put a touch of frost into my voice, the attitude of the busy and important man who wishes to be democratic but has had all the pushing around and hampering by underlings that he intends to put up with.

That did it. He said hastily, "I'm sure it's all right, Mr. Bonforte. It's just—well, regulations, you know."

"Yes, I know. Thank you." I started to push on through.

"Hold it, Mr. Bonforte! Look this way."

I glanced around. That *i*-dotting and *t*-crossing civil servant had held us up just long enough to let the press catch up with us. One man had dropped to his knee and was pointing a stereobox at me; he looked up and said, "Hold the wand where we can see it." Several others with various types of equipment were gathering around us; one had climbed up on the roof of the Rolls. Someone else was shoving a microphone at me and another had a directional mike aimed like a gun.

I was as angry as a leading woman with her name in small type but I remembered who I was supposed to be. I smiled and moved slowly. Bonforte had a good grasp of the fact that motion appears faster in pictures; I could afford to do it properly.

"Mr. Bonforte, why did you cancel the press conference?"

"Mr. Bonforte, it is asserted that you intend to demand that the Grand Assembly grant full Empire citizenship to Martians; will you comment?"

"Mr. Bonforte, how soon are you going to force a vote of confidence in the present government?"

I held up my hand with the wand in it and grinned. "One at a time, please! Now what was that first question?"

They all answered at once, of course; by the time they had sorted out precedence I had managed to waste several moments without having to answer anything. Bill Corpsman came charging up at that point. "Have a heart, boys. The Chief has had a hard day. I gave you all you need."

I held out a palm at him. "I can spare a minute or two, Bill. Gentlemen, I'm just about to leave but I'll try to cover the essentials of what you have asked. So far as I know the present government does not plan any reassessment of the relation of Mars to the Empire. Since I am not in office my own opinions are hardly pertinent. I suggest that you ask Mr. Quiroga. On the question of how soon the opposition will force a vote of confidence all I can say is that we won't do it unless we are sure we can win it—and you know as much about that as I do."

Someone said, "That doesn't say much, does it?"

"It was not intended to say much," I retorted, softening it with a grin. "Ask me questions I can legitimately answer and I will. Ask me those loaded 'Have-you-quit-beating-your-wife?' sort and I have answers to match." I hesitated, realizing that Bonforte had a reputation for bluntness and honesty, especially with the press. "But I am not trying to stall you. You all know why I am here today. Let me say this about it—and you can quote me if you wish." I reached back into my mind and hauled up an appropriate bit from the speeches of Bonforte I had studied. "The real meaning of what happened today is not that of an honor to one man. This"—I gestured with the Martian wand—"is proof that two great races can reach out across the gap of strangeness with understanding. Our own race is spreading out to the stars. We shall find—we *are* finding—that we are vastly outnumbered. If we are to succeed in our expansion to the stars, we must deal honestly, humbly, with open hearts. I have heard it said that our Martian neighbors would overrun

Earth if given the chance. This is nonsense; Earth is not suited to Martians. Let us protect our own—but let us not be seduced by fear and hatred into foolish acts. The stars will never be won by little minds; we must be big as space itself."

The reporter cocked an eyebrow. "Mr. Bonforte, seems to me I heard you make that speech last February."

"You will hear it next February. Also January, March, and all the other months. Truth cannot be too often repeated." I glanced back at the gatemaster and added, "I'm sorry but I'll have to go now—or I'll miss the tick." I turned and went through the gate, with Penny after me.

We climbed into the little lead-armored field car and the door sighed shut. The car was automatized, so I did not have to play up for a driver; I threw myself down and relaxed. "Whew!"

"I thought you did beautifully," Penny said seriously.

"I had a bad moment when he spotted the speech I was cribbing."

"You got away with it. It was an inspiration. You—you sounded just like *him*."

"Was there anybody there I should have called by name?"

"Not really. One or two maybe, but they wouldn't expect it when you were so rushed."

"I was caught in a squeeze. That fiddlin' gatemaster and his passports. Penny, I should think that you would carry them rather than Dak."

"Dak doesn't carry them. We all carry our own." She reached into her bag, pulled out a little book. "I had mine—but I did not dare admit it."

"Eh?"

"*He* had *his* on him when they got him. We haven't dared ask for a replacement—not at this time."

I was suddenly very weary.

Having no instructions from Dak or Rog, I stayed in character during the shuttle trip up and on entering the *Tom Paine*. It wasn't difficult; I simply went straight to the owner's cabin and spent long, miserable hours in free fall, biting my nails and wondering what was happening down on the surface. With the aid of anti-nausea pills I finally managed to float off into fitful sleep—which was a mistake, for I had a series of no-pants nightmares, with reporters pointing at me and cops touching me on the shoulder and Martians aiming their wands at me. They all knew I was phony and were simply arguing over who had the privilege of taking me apart and putting me down the oubliette.

I was awakened by the hooting of the acceleration alarm. Dak's vibrant baritone was booming, "First and last red warning! One third gee! One minute!" I hastily pulled myself

67

over to my bunk and held on. I felt lots better when it hit; one third gravity is not much, about the same as Mars' surface I think, but it is enough to steady the stomach and make the floor a real floor.

About five minutes later Dak knocked and let himself in as I was going to the door. "Howdy, Chief."

"Hello, Dak. I'm certainly glad to see you back."

"Not as glad as I am to be back," he said wearily. He eyed my bunk. "Mind if I spread out there?"

"Help yourself."

He did so and sighed. "Cripes, am I pooped! I could sleep for a week . . . I think I will."

"Let's both of us. Uh . . . You got him aboard?"

"Yes. What a gymkhana!"

"I suppose so. Still, it must be easier to do a job like that in a small, informal port like this than it was to pull the stunts you rigged at Jefferson."

"Huh? No, it's much harder here."

"Eh?"

"Obviously. Here everybody knows everybody—and people will talk." Dak smiled wryly. "We brought him aboard as a case of frozen canal shrimp. Had to pay export duty, too."

"Dak, how is he?"

"Well . . ." Dak frowned. "Doc Capek says that he will make a complete recovery—that it is just a matter of time." He added explosively, "If I could lay my hands on those rats! It would make you break down and bawl to see what they did to him—and yet we have to let them get away with it cold —for *his* sake."

Dak was fairly close to bawling himself. I said gently, "I gathered from Penny that they had roughed him up quite a lot. How badly is he hurt?"

"Huh? You must have misunderstood Penny. Aside from being filthy-dirty and needing a shave he was not hurt physically at all."

I looked stupid. "I thought they beat him up. Something about like working him over with a baseball bat."

"I would rather they had! Who cares about a few broken bones? No, no, it was what they did to his *brain.*"

"Oh . . ." I felt ill. "Brainwash?"

"Yes. Yes and no. They couldn't have been trying to make him talk because he didn't have any secrets that were of any possible political importance. He always operated out in the open and everybody knows it. They must have been using it simply to keep him under control, keep him from trying to escape."

He went on, "Doc says that he thinks they must have been using the minimum daily dose, just enough to keep him docile, until just before they turned him loose. Then they shot him with a load that would turn an elephant into a gibbering idiot. The front lobes of his brain must be soaked like a bath sponge."

I felt so ill that I was glad I had not eaten. I had once read up on the subject; I hate it so much that it fascinates me. To my mind there is something immoral and degrading in an absolute cosmic sense in tampering with a man's personality. Murder is a clean crime in comparison, a mere peccadillo. "Brainwash" is a term that comes down to us from the Communist movement of the Late Dark Ages; it was first applied to breaking a man's will and altering his personality by physical indignities and subtle torture. But that might take months; later they found a "better" way, one which would turn a man into a babbling slave in seconds—simply inject any one of several cocaine derivatives into his frontal brain lobes.

The filthy practice had first been developed for a legitimate purpose, to quiet disturbed patients and make them accessible to psychotherapy. As such, it was a humane advance, for it was used instead of lobotomy—"lobotomy" is a term almost as obsolete as "chastity girdle" but it means stirring a man's brain with a knife in such a fashion as to destroy his personality without killing him. Yes, they really used to do that—just as they used to beat them to "drive the devils out."

The Communists developed the new brainwash-by-drugs to an efficient technique, then when there were no more Communists, the Bands of Brothers polished it up still further until they could dose a man so lightly that he was simply receptive to leadership—or load him until he was a mindless mass of protoplasm—all in the sweet name of brotherhood. After all, you can't have "brotherhood" if a man is stubborn enough to want to keep his own secrets, can you? And what better way is there to be sure that he is not holding out on you than to poke a needle past his eyeball and slip a shot of babble juice into his brain? "You can't make an omelet without breaking eggs." The sophistries of villains—bah!

Of course, it has been illegal for a long, long time now, except for therapy, with the express consent of a court. But criminals use it and cops are sometimes not lily white, for it does make a prisoner talk and it does not leave any marks at all. The victim can even be told to forget that it has been done.

I knew most of this at the time Dak told me what had been done to Bonforte and the rest I cribbed out of the ship's Encyclopedia Batavia. See the article on "Psychic Integration" and the one on "Torture."

I shook my head and tried to put the nightmares out of my mind. "But he's going to recover?"

"Doc says that the drug does not alter the brain structure; it just paralyzes it. He says that eventually the blood stream picks up and carries away all of the dope; it reaches the kidneys and passes out of the body. But it takes time." Dak looked up at me. "Chief?"

"Eh? About time to knock off that 'Chief' stuff, isn't it? He's back."

"That's what I wanted to talk to you about. Would it be too much trouble to you to keep up the impersonation just a little while longer?"

"But why? There's nobody here but just us chickens."

"That's not quite true. Lorenzo, we've managed to keep this secret awfully tight. There's me, there's you." He ticked it off on his fingers. "There's Doc and Rog and Bill. And Penny, of course. There's a man by the name of Langston back Earthside whom you've never met. I think Jimmie Washington suspects but he wouldn't tell his own mother the right time of day. We don't know how many took part in the kidnaping, but not many, you can be sure. In any case, *they* don't dare talk—and the joke of it is they no longer could prove that he had ever been missing even if they wanted to. But my point is this: here in the *Tommie* we've got all the crew and all the idlers not in on it. Old son, how about staying with it and letting yourself be seen each day by crewmen and by Jimmie Washington's girl and such—while *he* gets well? Huh?"

"Mmm . . . I don't see why not. How long will it be?"

"Just the trip back. We'll take it slow, at an easy boost. You'll enjoy it."

"Okay. Dak, don't figure this into my fee. I'm doing this piece of it just because I *hate* brainwashing."

Dak bounced up and clapped me on the shoulder. "You're my kind of people, Lorenzo. Don't worry about your fee; you'll be taken care of." His manner changed. "Very well, Chief. See you in the morning, sir."

But one thing leads to another. The boost we had started on Dak's return was a mere shift of orbits, to one farther out where there would be little chance of a news service sending up a shuttle for a follow-up story. I woke up in free fall, took a pill, and managed to eat breakfast. Penny showed up shortly thereafter. "Good morning, Mr. Bonforte."

"Good morning, Penny." I inclined my head in the direction of the guest room. "Any news?"

"No, sir. About the same. Captain's compliments and would it be too much trouble for you to come to his cabin?"

"Not at all." Penny followed me in. Dak was there, with his heels hooked to his chair to stay in place; Rog and Bill were strapped to the couch.

Dak looked around and said, "Thanks for coming in, Chief. We need some help."

"Good morning. What is it?"

Clifton answered my greeting with his usual dignified deference and called me Chief; Corpsman nodded. Dak went on, "To clean this up in style you should make one more appearance."

"Eh? I thought——"

"Just a second. The networks were led to expect a major speech from you today, commenting on yesterday's event. I thought Rog intended to cancel it, but Bill has the speech worked up. Question is, will you deliver it?"

The trouble with adopting a cat is that they always have kittens. "Where? Goddard City?"

"Oh no. Right in your cabin. We beam it to Phobos; they can it for Mars and also put it on the high circuit for New Batavia, where the Earth nets will pick it up and where it will be relayed for Venus, Ganymede, et cetera. Inside of four hours it will be all over the system but you'll never have to stir out of your cabin."

There is something very tempting about a grand network. I had never been on one but once and that time my act got clipped down to the point where my face showed for only twenty-seven seconds. But to have one all to myself——

Dak thought I was reluctant and added, "It won't be a strain, as we are equipped to can it right here in the *Tommie*. Then we can project it first and clip out anything if necessary."

"Well—all right. You have the script, Bill?"

"Yes."

"Let me check it."

"What do you mean? You'll have it in plenty of time."

"Isn't that it in your hand?"

"Well, yes."

"Then let me read it."

Corpsman looked annoyed. "You'll have it an hour before we record. These things go better if they sound spontaneous."

"Sounding spontaneous is a matter of careful preparation, Bill. It's my trade. I know."

"You did all right at the skyfield yesterday without rehearsal. This is just more of the same old hoke: I want you to do it the same way."

Bonforte's personality was coming through stronger the longer Corpsman stalled; I think Clifton could see that I

71

was about to cloud up and storm, for he said, "Oh, for Pete's sake, Bill! Hand him the speech."

Corpsman snorted and threw the sheets at me. In free fall they sailed but the air spread them wide. Penny gathered them together, sorted them, and gave them to me. I thanked her, said nothing more, and started to read.

I skimmed through it in a fraction of the time it would take to deliver it. Finally I finished and looked up.

"Well?" said Rog.

"About five minutes of this concerns the adoption. The rest is an argument for the policies of the Expansionist Party. Pretty much the same as I've heard in the speeches you've had me study."

"Yes," agreed Clifton. "The adoption is the hook we hang the rest on. As you know, we expect to force a vote of confidence before long."

"I understand. You can't miss this chance to beat the drum. Well, it's all right, but——"

"But what? What's worrying you?"

"Well—characterization. In several places the wording should be changed. It's not the way *he* would express it."

Corpsman exploded with a word unnecessary in the presence of a lady; I gave him a cold glance. "Now see here, Smythe," he went on, "who knows how Bonforte would say it? You? Or the man who has been writing his speeches the past four years?"

I tried to keep my temper; he had a point. "It is nevertheless the case," I answered, "that a line which looks okay in print may not deliver well. Mr. Bonforte is a great orator, I have already learned. He belongs with Webster, Churchill, and Demosthenes—a rolling grandeur expressed in simple words. Now take this word 'intransigent,' which you have used twice. I might say that, but I have a weakness for polysyllables; I like to exhibit my literary erudition. But Mr. Bonforte would say 'stubborn' or 'mulish' or 'pigheaded.' The reason he would is, naturally, that they convey emotion much more effectively."

"You see that you make the delivery effective! I'll worry about the words."

"You don't understand, Bill. I don't care whether the speech is politically effective or not; my job is to carry out a characterization. I can't do that if I put into the mouth of the character words that he would never use; it would sound as forced and phony as a goat spouting Greek. But if I read the speech in words he *would* use, it will automatically be effective. He's a great orator."

"Listen, Smythe, you're not hired to write speeches. You're hired to——"

"Hold it, Bill!" Dak cut in. "And a little less of that 'Smythe' stuff, too. Well, Rog? How about it?"

Clifton said, "As I understand it, Chief, your only objection is to some of the phrasing?"

"Well, yes. I'd suggest cutting out that personal attack on Mr. Quiroga, too, and the insinuation about his financial backers. It doesn't sound like real Bonforte to me."

He looked sheepish. "That's a bit I put in myself. But you may be right. He always gives a man the benefit of the doubt." He remained silent for a moment. "You make the changes you think you have to. We'll can it and look at the playback. We can always clip it—or even cancel completely 'due to technical difficulties.'" He smiled grimly. "That's what we'll do, Bill."

"Damn it, this is a ridiculous example of——"

"That's how it is going to be, Bill."

Corpsman left the room very suddenly. Clifton sighed. "Bill always has hated the notion that anybody but Mr. B. could give him instructions. But he's an able man. Uh, Chief, how soon can you be ready to record? We patch in at sixteen hundred."

"I don't know. I'll be ready in time."

Penny followed me back into my office. When she closed the door I said, "I won't need you for the next hour or so, Penny child. But you might ask Doc for more of those pills. I may need them."

"Yes, sir." She floated with her back to the door. "Chief?"

"Yes, Penny?"

"I just wanted to say don't believe what Bill said about writing his speeches!"

"I didn't. I've heard his speeches—and I've read this."

"Oh, Bill does submit drafts, lots of times. So does Rog. I've even done it myself. He—*he* will use ideas from anywhere if he thinks they are good. But when he delivers a speech, it is *his,* every word of it."

"I believe you. I wish he had written this one ahead of time."

"You just do your best!"

I did. I started out simply substituting synonyms, putting in the gutty Germanic words in place of the "intestinal" Latin jawbreakers. Then I got excited and red in the face and tore it to pieces. It's a lot of fun for an actor to mess around with lines; he doesn't get the chance very often.

I used no one but Penny for my audience and made sure from Dak that I was not being tapped elsewhere in the ship—though I suspect that the big-boned galoot cheated on me and listened in himself. I had Penny in tears in the first three minutes; by the time I finished (twenty-eight and a half minutes, just time for station announcements, she was limp). I took no liberties with the straight Expansionist doctrine, as proclaimed by its official prophet, the Right Honorable John Joseph Bonforte; I simply reconstructed his message and his delivery, largely out of phrases from other speeches.

Here's an odd thing—I believed every word of it while I was talking.

But, brother, I made a speech!

Afterwards we all listened to the playback, complete with full stereo of myself. Jimmie Washington was present, which kept Bill Corpsman quiet. When it was over I said, "How about it, Rog? Do we need to clip anything?"

He took his cigar out of his mouth and said, "No. If you want my advice, Chief, I'd say to let it go as it is."

Corpsman left the room again—but Mr. Washington came over with tears leaking out of his eyes—tears are a nuisance in free fall; there's nowhere for them to go. "Mr. Bonforte, that was *beautiful*."

"Thanks, Jimmie."

Penny could not talk at all.

I turned in after that; a top-notch performance leaves me fagged. I slept for more than eight hours, then was awakened by the hooter. I had strapped myself to my bunk—I hate to float around while sleeping in free fall—so I did not have to move. But I had not known that we were getting under way so I called the control room between first and second warning. "Captain Broadbent?"

"Just a moment, sir," I heard Epstein answer.

Then Dak's voice came over. "Yes, Chief? We are getting under way on schedule—pursuant to your orders."

"Eh? Oh yes, certainly."

"I believe Mr. Clifton is on his way to your cabin."

"Very well, Captain." I lay back and waited.

Immediately after we started to boost at one gee Rog Clifton came in; he had a worried look on his face I could not interpret—equal parts of triumph, worry, and confusion. "What is it, Rog?"

"Chief! They've jumped the gun on us! The Quiroga government has resigned!"

7

I was still logy with sleep; I shook my head to try to clear it. "What are you in such a spin about, Rog? That's what you were trying to accomplish, wasn't it?"

"Well, yes, of course. But——" He stopped.

"But what? I don't get it. Here you chaps have been working and scheming for years to bring about this very thing. Now you've won—and you look like a bride who isn't sure she wants to go through with it. Why? The no-good-nicks are out and now God's chillun get their innings. No?"

"Uh—you haven't been in politics much."

"You know I haven't. I got trimmed when I ran for patrol leader in my scout troop. That cured me."

"Well, you see, timing is everything."

"So my father always told me. Look here, Rog, do I gather that if you had your druthers you'd druther Quiroga was still in office? You said he had 'jumped the gun.' "

"Let me explain. What we really wanted was to move a vote of confidence and win it, and thereby force a general election on them—but at our own time, when we estimated that we could win the election."

"Oh. And you don't figure you can win now? You think Quiroga will go back into office for another five years—or at least the Humanity Party will?"

Clifton looked thoughtful. "No, I think our chances are pretty good to win the election."

"Eh? Maybe I'm not awake yet. Don't you *want* to win?"

"Of course. But don't you see what this resignation has done to us?"

"I guess I don't."

"Well, the government in power can order a general election at any time up to the constitutional limitation of five years. Ordinarily they will go to the people when the time seems most favorable to them. But they don't resign between the announcement and the election unless forced to. You follow me?"

I realized that the event did seem odd, little attention as I paid to politics. "I believe so."

"But in this case Quiroga's government scheduled a general election, then resigned in a body, leaving the Empire

75

without a government. Therefore the sovereign must call on someone else to form a 'caretaker' government to serve until the election. By the letter of the law he can ask any member of the Grand Assembly, but as a matter of strict constitutional precedent he has no choice. When a government resigns in a body—not just reshuffling portfolios but quits as a whole—then the sovereign *must* call on the leader of the opposition to form the 'caretaker' government. It's indispensable to our system; it keeps resigning from being just a gesture. Many other methods have been tried in the past; under some of them governments were changed as often as underwear. But our present system insures responsible government."

I was so busy trying to see the implications that I almost missed his next remark. "So, naturally, the Emperor has summoned Mr. Bonforte to New Batavia."

"Eh? New Batavia? Well!" I was thinking that I had never seen the Imperial capital. The one time I had been on the Moon the vicissitudes of my profession had left me without time or money for the side trip. "Then that is why we got under way? Well, I certainly don't mind. I suppose you can always find a way to send me home if the *Tommie* doesn't go back to Earth soon."

"What? Good heavens, don't worry about that now. When the time comes, Captain Broadbent can find any number of ways to deliver you home."

"Sorry. I forget that you have more important matters on your mind, Rog. Sure, I'm anxious to get home now that the job is done. But a few days, or even a month, on Luna would not matter. I have nothing pressing me. But thanks for taking time to tell me the news." I searched his face. "Rog, you look worried as hell."

"Don't you see? The Emperor has sent for Mr. Bonforte. The *Emperor*, man! And Mr. Bonforte is in no shape to appear at an audience. They have risked a gambit—and perhaps trapped us in a checkmate!"

"Eh? Now wait a minute. Slow up. I see what you are driving at—but, look, friend, we aren't at New Batavia. We're a hundred million miles away, or two hundred million, or whatever it is. Doc Capek will have him wrung out and ready to speak his piece by then. Won't he?"

"Well—we hope so."

"But you aren't sure?"

"We can't be sure. Capek says that there is little clinical data on such massive doses. It depends on the individual's body chemistry and on the exact drug used."

I suddenly remembered a time when an understudy had slipped me a powerful purgative just before a performance.

(But I went on anyhow, which proves the superiority of mind over matter—then I got him fired.) "Rog—they gave him that last, unnecessarily big dose not just out of simple sadism—but to set up this situation!"

"*I* think so. So does Capek."

"Hey! In that case it would mean that Quiroga himself is the man behind the kidnaping—and that we've had a *gangster* running the Empire!"

Rog shook his head. "Not necessarily. Not even probably. But it would indeed mean that the same forces who control the Actionists also control the machinery of the Humanity Party. But you will never pin anything on *them;* they are unreachable, ultrarespectable. Nevertheless, they could send word to Quiroga that the time had come to roll over and play dead—and have him do it. Almost certainly," he added, "without giving him a hint of the real reason why the moment was timely."

"Criminy! Do you mean to tell me that the top man in the Empire would fold up and quit, just like that? Because somebody behind the scenes ordered him to?"

"I'm afraid that is just what I do think."

I shook my head. "Politics is a dirty game!"

"No," Clifton answered insistently. "There is no such thing as a dirty game. But you sometimes run into dirty players."

"I don't see the difference."

"There is a world of difference. Quiroga is a third-rater and a stooge—in my opinion, a stooge for villains. But there is nothing third-rate about John Joseph Bonforte and he has never, *ever* been a stooge for anyone. As a follower, he believed in the cause; as the leader, he has led from conviction!"

"I stand corrected," I said humbly. "Well, what do we do? Have Dak drag his feet so that the *Tommie* does not reach New Batavia until he is back in shape to do the job?"

"We *can't* stall. We don't have to boost at more than one gravity; nobody would expect a man Bonforte's age to place unnecessary strain on his heart. But we can't delay. When the Emperor sends for you, you come."

"Then what?"

Rog looked at me without answering. I began to get edgy. "Hey, Rog, don't go getting any wild notions! This hasn't anything to do with *me.* I'm through, except for a few casual appearances around the ship. Dirty or not, politics is not my game—just pay me off and ship me home and I'll guarantee never even to register to vote!"

"You probably wouldn't have to do anything. Dr. Capek will almost certainly have him in shape for it. But it isn't as if it were anything *hard*—not like that adoption ceremony —just an audience with the Emperor and——"

"The Emperor!" I almost screamed. Like most Americans, I did not understand royalty, did not really approve of the institution in my heart—and had a sneaking, unadmitted awe of kings. After all, we Americans came in by the back door. When we swapped associate status under treaty for the advantages of a full voice in the affairs of the Empire, it was explicitly agreed that our local institutions, our own constitution, and so forth, would not be affected—and tacitly agreed that no member of the royal family would ever visit America. Maybe that is a bad thing. Maybe if we were used to royalty we would not be so impressed by them. In any case, it is notorious that "democratic" American women are more quiveringly anxious to be presented at court than is anybody else.

"Now take it easy," Rog answered. "You probably won't have to do it at all. We just want to be prepared. What I was trying to tell you is that a 'caretaker' government is no problem. It passes no laws, changes no policies. I'll take care of all the work. All you will have to do—if you have to do anything—is make the formal appearance before King Willem—and possibly show up at a controlled press conference or two, depending on how long it is before *he* is well again. What you have already done is much harder—and you will be paid whether we need you or not."

"Damn it, pay has nothing to do with it! It's—well, in the words of a famous character in theatrical history, 'Include me *out*.'"

Before Rog could answer, Bill Corpsman came bursting into my cabin without knocking, looked at us, and said sharply to Clifton, "Have you told him?"

"Yes," agreed Clifton. "He's turned down the job."

"Huh? Nonsense!"

"It's not nonsense," I answered, "and by the way, Bill, that door you just came through has a nice spot on it to knock. In the profession the custom is to knock and shout, 'Are you decent?' I wish you would remember it."

"Oh, dirty sheets! We're in a hurry. What's this guff about your refusing?"

"It's not guff. This is not the job I signed up for."

"Garbage! Maybe you are too stupid to realize it, Smythe, but you are in too deep to prattle about backing out. It wouldn't be healthy."

I went to him and grabbed his arm. "Are you threatening me? If you are, let's go outside and talk it over."

He shook my hand off. "In a spaceship? You really are

78

simple, aren't you? But haven't you got it through your thick head that you caused this mess yourself?"

"What do you mean?"

"He means," Clifton answered, "that he is convinced that the fall of the Quiroga government was the direct result of the speech you made earlier today. It is even possible that he is right. But it is beside the point. Bill, try to be reasonably polite, will you? We get nowhere by bickering."

I was so surprised by the suggestion that *I* had caused Quiroga to resign that I forgot all about my desire to loosen Corpsman's teeth. Were they serious? Sure, it was one dilly of a fine speech, but was such a result possible?

Well, if it was, it was certainly fast service.

I said wonderingly, "Bill, do I understand that you are complaining that the speech I made was too effective to suit you?"

"Huh? Hell, no! It was a lousy speech."

"So? You can't have it both ways. You're saying that a lousy speech went over so big that it scared the Humanity Party right out of office. Is that what you meant?"

Corpsman looked annoyed, started to answer, and caught sight of Clifton suppressing a grin. He scowled, again started to reply—finally shrugged and said, "All right, buster, you proved your point; the speech could not have had anything to do with the fall of the Quiroga government. Nevertheless, we've got work to do. So what's this about you not being willing to carry your share of the load?"

I looked at him and managed to keep my temper—Bonforte's influence again; playing the part of a calm-tempered character tends to make one calm inside. "Bill, again you cannot have it two ways. You have made it emphatically clear that you consider me just a hired hand. Therefore I have no obligation beyond my job, which is finished. You can't hire me for another job unless it suits me. It doesn't."

He started to speak but I cut in. "That's all. Now get out. You're not welcome here."

He looked astounded. "Who the hell do you think you are to give orders around here?"

"Nobody. Nobody at all, as you have pointed out. But this is my private room, assigned to me by the Captain. So now get out or be thrown out. I don't like your manners."

Clifton added quietly, "Clear out, Bill. Regardless of anything else, it is his private cabin at the present time. So you had better leave." Rog hesitated, then added, "I think we both might as well leave; we don't seem to be getting anywhere. If you will excuse us—Chief?"

"Certainly."

I sat and thought about it for several minutes. I was

sorry that I had let Corpsman provoke me even into such a mild exchange; it lacked dignity. But I reviewed it in my mind and assured myself that my personal differences with Corpsman had not affected my decision; my mind had been made up before he appeared.

A sharp knock came at the door. I called out, "Who is it?"

"Captain Broadbent."

"Come in, Dak."

He did so, sat down, and for some minutes seemed interested only in pulling hangnails. Finally he looked up and said, "Would it change your mind if I slapped the blighter in the brig?"

"Eh? Do you have a brig in the ship?"

"No. But it would not be hard to jury-rig one."

I looked at him sharply, trying to figure what went on inside that bony head. "Would you actually put Bill in the brig if I asked for it?"

He looked up, cocked a brow, and grinned wryly. "No. A man doesn't get to be a captain operating on any such basis as that. I would not take that sort of order even from *him*." He inclined his head toward the room Bonforte was in. "Certain decisions a man must make himself."

"That's right."

"Mmm—I hear you've made one of that sort."

"That's right."

"So. I've come to have a lot of respect for you, old son. First met you, I figured you for a clotheshorse and a facemaker, with nothing inside. I was wrong."

"Thank you."

"So I won't plead with you. Just tell me: is it worth our time to discuss the factors? Have you given it plenty of thought?"

"My mind is made up, Dak. This isn't my pidgin."

"Well, perhaps you're right. I'm sorry. I guess we'll just have to hope he pulls out of it in time." He stood up. "By the way, Penny would like to see you, if you aren't going to turn in again this minute."

I laughed without pleasure. "Just 'by the way,' eh? Is this the proper sequence? Isn't it Dr. Capek's turn to try to twist my arm?"

"He skipped his turn; he's busy with Mr. B. He sent you a message, though."

"Eh?"

"He said you could go to hell. Embroidered it a bit, but that was the gist."

"He did? Well, tell him I'll save him a seat by the fire."

"Can Penny come in?"

"Oh, sure! But you can tell her that she is wasting her time; the answer is still 'No.' "

So I changed my mind. Confound it, why should an argument seem so much more logical when underlined with a whiff of Jungle Lust? Not that Penny used unfair means, she did not even shed tears—not that I laid a finger on her —but I found myself conceding points, and presently there were no more points to concede. There is no getting around it, Penny is the world-saver type and her sincerity is contagious.

The boning I did on the trip out to Mars was as nothing to the hard study I put in on the trip to New Batavia. I already had the basic character; now it was necessary to fill in the background, prepare myself to *be* Bonforte under almost any circumstances. While it was the royal audience I was aiming at, once we were at New Batavia I might have to meet any of hundreds or thousands of people. Rog planned to give me a defense in depth of the sort that is routine for any public figure if he is to get work done; nevertheless, I would have to see people—a public figure is a public figure, no way to get around that.

The tightrope act I was going to have to attempt was made possible only by Bonforte's Farleyfile, perhaps the best one ever compiled. Farley was a political manager of the twentieth century, of Eisenhower I believe, and the method he invented for handling the personal relations of politics was as revolutionary as the German invention of staff command was to warfare. Yet I had never heard of the device until Penny showed me Bonforte's.

It was nothing but a file about people. However, the art of politics is "nothing but" people. This file contained all, or almost all, of the thousands upon thousands of people Bonforte had met in the course of his long public life; each dossier consisted of what he knew about that person *from Bonforte's own personal contact*. Anything at all, no matter how trivial—in fact, trivia were always the first entries: names and nicknames of wives, children, and pets, hobbies, tastes in food or drink, prejudices, eccentricities. Following this would be listed date and place and comments for *every occasion* on which Bonforte had talked to that particular man.

When available, a photo was included. There might or might not be "below-the-line" data, i.e. information which had been researched rather than learned directly by Bonforte. It depended on the political importance of the person. In some cases the "below-the-line" part was a formal biography running to thousands of words.

Both Penny and Bonforte himself carried minicorders powered by their body heat. If Bonforte was alone he would dictate into his own when opportunity offered—in rest rooms, while riding, etc.; if Penny went along she would take it down in hers, which was disguised to look like a wrist watch. Penny could not possibly do the transcribing and microfilming; two of Jimmie Washington's girls did little else.

When Penny showed me the Farleyfile, showed me the very bulk of it—and it was bulky, even at ten thousand words or more to the spool—and then told me that this represented personal information about Mr. Bonforte's acquaintances, I scroaned (which is a scream and groan done together, with intense feeling). "God's mercy, child! I tried to tell you this job could not be done. How could anyone memorize all that?"

"Why, you can't, of course."

"You just said that this was what *he* remembered about his friends and acquaintances."

"Not quite. I said that this is what he wanted to remember. But since he can't, not possibly, this is how he does it. Don't worry; you don't have to memorize anything. I just want you to know that it is available. It is my job to see that he has at least a minute or two to study the appropriate Farleyfile before anybody gets in to see him. If the need turns up, I can protect you with the same service."

I looked at the typical file she had projected on the desk reader. A Mr. Saunders of Pretoria, South Africa, I believe it was. He had a bulldog named Snuffles Bullyboy, several assorted uninteresting offspring, and he liked a twist of lime in his whisky and splash. "Penny, do you mean to tell me that Mr. B. pretends to remember minutiae like that? It strikes me as rather phony."

Instead of getting angry at the slur on her idol Penny nodded soberly. "I thought so once. But you don't look at it correctly, Chief. Do you ever write down the telephone number of a friend?"

"Eh? Of course."

"Is it dishonest? Do you apologize to your friend for caring so little about him that you can't simply remember his number?"

"*Eh?* All right, I give up. You've sold me."

"These are things he would like to remember if his memory were perfect. Since it isn't, it is no more phony to do it this way than it is to use a tickler file in order not to forget a friend's birthday—that's what it is: a giant tickler file, to cover *anything*. But there is more to it. Did you ever meet a really important person?"

I tried to think. Penny did not mean the greats of the

theatrical profession; she hardly knew they existed. "I once met President Warfield. I was a kid of ten or eleven."

"Do you remember the details?"

"Why, certainly. He said, 'How did you break that arm, son?' and I said, 'Riding a bicycle, sir,' and he said, 'Did the same thing myself, only it was a collarbone.'"

"Do you think he would remember it if he were still alive?"

"Why, no."

"He might—he may have had you Farleyfiled. This Farleyfile includes boys of that age, because boys grow up and become men. The point is that top-level men like President Warfield meet many more people than they can remember. Each one of that faceless throng remembers his own meeting with the famous man and remembers it in detail. But the supremely important person in any one's life is *himself*—and a politician must never forget that. So it is polite and friendly and warmhearted for the politician to have a way to be able to remember about other people the sort of little things that they are likely to remember about him. It is also essential—in politics."

I had Penny display the Farleyfile on King Willem. It was rather short, which dismayed me at first, until I concluded that it meant that Bonforte did not know the Emperor well and had met him only on a few official occasions—Bonforte's first service as Supreme Minister had been before old Emperor Frederick's death. There was no biography below the line, but just a notation, *"See* House of Orange." I didn't —there simply wasn't time to plow through a few million words of Empire and pre-Empire history and, anyhow, I got fair-to-excellent marks in history when I was in school. All I wanted to know about the Emperor was what Bonforte knew about him that other people did not.

It occurred to me that the Farleyfile must include everybody in the ship since they were (a) people (b) whom Bonforte had met. I asked Penny for them. She seemed a little surprised.

Soon I was the one surprised. The *Tom Paine* had in her *six* Grand Assemblymen. Rog Clifton and Mr. Bonforte, of course—but the first item in Dak's file read: "Broadbent, Darius K., the Honorable, G. A. for League of Free Travelers, Upper Division." It also mentioned that he held a Ph.D. in physics, had been reserve champion with the pistol in the Imperial Matches nine years earlier, and had published three volumes of verse under the nom de plume of "Acey Wheelwright." I resolved never again to take a man at merely his face value.

There was a notation in Bonforte's sloppy handwriting: "Almost irresistible to women—and vice versa!"

Penny and Dr. Capek were also members of the great parliament. Even Jimmie Washington was a member, for a "safe" district, I realized later—he represented the Lapps, including all the reindeer and Santa Claus, no doubt. He was also ordained in the First Bible Truth Church of the Holy Spirit, which I had never heard of, but which accounted for his tight-lipped deacon look.

I especially enjoyed reading about Penny—the Honorable Miss Penelope Taliaferro Russell. She was an M.A. in government administration from Georgetown and a B.A. from Wellesley, which somehow did not surprise me. She represented districtless university women, another "safe" constituency (I learned) since they are about five to one Expansionist Party members.

On down below were her glove size, her other measurements, her preferences in colors (I could teach her something about dressing), her preference in scent (Jungle Lust, of course), and many other details, most of them innocuous enough. But there was "comment":

"Neurotically honest—arithmetic unreliable—prides herself on her sense of humor, or which she has none—watches her diet but is gluttonous about candied cherries—little-mother-of-all-living complex—unable to resist reading the printed word in any form."

Underneath was another of Bonforte's handwritten addenda: "Ah, Curly Top! Snooping again, I see."

As I turned them back to her I asked Penny if she had read her own Farleyfile. She told me snippily to mind my own business! Then turned red and apologized.

Most of my time was taken up with study but I did take time to review and revise carefully the physical resemblance, checking the Semiperm shading by colorimeter, doing an extremely careful job on the wrinkles, adding two moles, and setting the whole job with electric brush. It was going to mean a skin peel before I could get my own face back but that was a small price to pay for a make-up job that could not be damaged, could not be smeared even with acetone, and was proof against such hazards as napkins. I even added the scar on the "game" leg, using a photograph Capek had kept in Bonforte's health history. If Bonforte had had wife or mistress, she would have had difficulty in telling the impostor from the real thing simply on physical appearance. It was a lot of trouble but it left my mind free to worry about the really difficult part of the impersonation.

But the all-out effort during the trip was to steep myself

in what Bonforte thought and believed, in short the policies of the Expansionist Party. In a manner of speaking, he himself was the Expansionist Party, not merely its most prominent leader but its political philosopher and greatest statesman. Expansionism had hardly been more than a "Manifest Destiny" movement when the party was founded, a rabble coalition of groups who had one thing in common: the belief that the frontiers in the sky were the most important issue in the emerging future of the human race. Bonforte had given the party a rationale and an ethic, the theme that freedom and equal rights must run with the Imperial banner; he kept harping on the notion that the human race must never again make the mistakes that the white subrace had made in Africa and Asia.

But I was confused by the fact—I was awfully unsophisticated in such matters—that the early history of the Expansionist Party sounded remarkably like the present Humanity Party. I was not aware that political parties often change as much in growing up as people do. I had known vaguely that the Humanity Party had started as a splinter of the Expansionist movement but I had never thought about it. Actually it was inevitable; as the political parties which did not have their eyes on the sky dwindled away under the imperatives of history and ceased to elect candidates, the one party which had been on the right track was bound to split into two factions.

But I am running ahead; my political education did not proceed so logically. At first I simply soaked myself in Bonforte's public utterances. True, I had done that on the trip out, but then I was studying how he spoke; now I was studying what he said.

Bonforte was an orator in the grand tradition but he could be vitriolic in debate, e.g. a speech he made in New Paris during the ruckus over the treaty with the Martian nests, the Concord of Tycho. It was this treaty which had knocked him out of office before; he had pushed it through but the strain on the coalition had lost him the next vote of confidence. Nevertheless, Quiroga had not dared denounce the treaty. I listened to this speech with special interest since I had not liked the treaty myself; the idea that Martians must be granted the same privileges on Earth that humans enjoyed on Mars had been abhorrent to me—until I visited the Kkkah nest.

"My opponent," Bonforte had said with a rasp in his voice, "would have you believe that the motto of the so-called Humanity Party, 'Government of human beings, by human beings, and for human beings,' is no more than an updating of the immortal words of Lincoln. But while the voice is the voice of Abraham, the hand is the hand of the Ku Klux Klan. The true meaning of that innocent-seeming motto is 'Government of all races everywhere, by human beings alone, for the profit of a privileged few.'

"But, my opponent protests, we have a God-given mandate to spread enlightenment through the stars, dispensing our own brand of Civilization to the savages. This is the Uncle Remus school of sociology—the good dahkies singin' spirituals and Ole Massa lubbin' every one of dem! It is a beautiful picture but the frame is too small; it fails to show the whip, the slave block—and the counting house!"

I found myself becoming, if not an Expansionist, then at least a Bonfortite. I am not sure that I was convinced by the logic of his words—indeed, I am not sure that they were logical. But I was in a receptive frame of mind. I wanted to understand what he said so thoroughly that I could rephrase it and say it in his place, if need be.

Nevertheless, here was a man who knew what he wanted and (much rarer!) why he wanted it. I could not help but be impressed, and it forced me to examine my own beliefs. What did I live by?

My profession, surely! I had been brought up in it, I liked it, I had a deep though unlogical conviction that art was worth the effort—and, besides, it was the only way I knew to make a living. But what else?

I have never been impressed by the formal schools of ethics. I had sampled them—public libraries are a ready source of recreation for an actor short of cash—but I had found them as poor in vitamins as a mother-in-law's kiss. Given time and plenty of paper, a philosopher can prove anything.

I had the same contempt for the moral instruction handed to most children. Much of it is prattle and the parts they really seem to mean are dedicated to the sacred proposition that a "good" child is one who does not disturb mother's nap and a "good" man is one who achieves a muscular bank account without getting caught. No, thanks!

But even a dog has rules of conduct. What were mine? How did I behave—or, at least, how did I like to think I behaved?

"The show must go on." I had always believed that and lived by it. But why must the show go on?—seeing that some shows are pretty terrible. Well, because you agreed to do it, because there is an audience out there; they have paid and each one of them is entitled to the best you can give. You owe it to them. You owe it also to stagehands and manager and producer and other members of the company— and to those who taught you your trade, and to others stretching back in history to open-air theaters and stone seats and even to storytellers squatting in a market place. *Noblesse oblige.*

I decided that the notion could be generalized into any occupation. "Value for value." Building "on the square and on the level." The Hippocratic oath. Don't let the team down. Honest work for honest pay. Such things did not have to be proved; they were an essential part of life—true throughout eternity, true in the farthest reaches of the Galaxy.

I suddenly got a glimpse of what Bonforte was driving at. If there were ethical basics that transcended time and place, then they were true both for Martians and for men. They were true on any planet around any star—and if the human race did not behave accordingly they weren't ever going to win to the stars because some better race would slap them down for double-dealing.

The price of expansion was virtue. "Never give a sucker an even break" was too narrow a philosophy to fit the broad reaches of space.

But Bonforte was not preaching sweetness and light. "I am not a pacifist. Pacifism is a shifty doctrine under which a man accepts the benefits of the social group without being willing to pay—and claims a halo for his dishonesty. Mr. Speaker, life belongs to those who do not fear to lose it. This bill must pass!" And with that he had got up and crossed the aisle in support of a military appropriation his own party had refused in caucus.

Or again: "Take sides! Always take sides! You will sometimes be wrong—but the man who refuses to take sides must *always* be wrong! Heaven save us from poltroons who fear to make a choice. Let us stand up and be counted." (This last was in a closed caucus but Penny had caught it on her minicorder and Bonforte had saved it—Bonforte had a sense of history; he was a record keeper. If he had not been, I would not have had much to work with.)

I decided that Bonforte was my kind of man. Or at least the kind I liked to think I was. His was a *persona* I was proud to wear.

So far as I can remember I did not sleep on that trip after I promised Penny that I would take the royal audience if Bonforte could not be made ready. I intended to sleep—there is no point in taking your stage with your eyes bagging like hound's ears—but I got interested in what I was studying and there was a plentiful supply of pepper pills in Bonforte's desk. It is amazing how much ground you can cover working a twenty-four-hour day, free from interruptions and with all the help you could ask for.

But shortly before we were due at New Batavia, Dr. Capek came in and said, "Bare your left forearm."

"Why?" I asked.

"Because when you go before the Emperor we don't want you falling flat on your face with fatigue. This will make you sleep until we ground. Then I'll give you an antidote."

"Eh? I take it that you don't think *he* will be ready?"

Capek did not answer, but gave me the shot. I tried to finish listening to the speech I was running but I must have been asleep in seconds. The next thing I knew Dak was saying deferentially, "Wake up, sir. Please wake up. We're grounded at Lippershey Field."

8

Our Moon being an airless planet, a torchship can land on it. But the *Tom Paine,* being a torchship, was really intended to stay in space and be serviced only at space stations in orbit; she had to be landed in a cradle. I wish I had been awake to see it, for they say that catching an egg on a plate is easy by comparison. Dak was one of the half dozen pilots who could do it.

But I did not even get to see the *Tommie* in her cradle; all I saw was the inside of the passenger bellows they fastened to her air lock and the passenger tube to New Batavia —those tubes are so fast that, under the low gravity of the Moon, you are again in free fall at the middle of the trip.

We went first to the apartments assigned to the leader of the loyal opposition, Bonforte's official residence until (and if) he went back into power after the coming election. The magnificence of them made me wonder what the Supreme Minister's residence was like. I suppose that New Batavia is odds-on the most palatial capital city in all history; it is a shame that it can hardly be seen from outdoors—but that minor shortcoming is more than offset by the fact that it is the only city in the Solar System that is actually impervious to fusion bombs. Or perhaps I should say "effectively impervious" since there are some surface structures which could be destroyed. Bonforte's apartments included an upper living room in the side of a cliff, which looked out through a bubble balcony at the stars and Mother Earth herself—but his sleeping room and offices were a thousand feet of solid rock below, by private lift.

I had no time to explore the apartments; they dressed me for the audience. Bonforte had no valet even dirtside, but Rog insisted on "helping" me (he was a hindrance) while going over last-minute details. The dress was ancient formal court dress, shapeless tubular trousers, a silly jacket with a claw-hammer tail, both in black, and a chemise consisting of a stiff white breastplate, a "winged" collar, and a white bow tie. Bonforte's chemise was all in one piece, because (I suppose) he did not use a dresser; correctly it should be assembled piece by piece and the bow tie should be tied poorly enough to show that it has been tied by hand—but it is too much to expect a man to understand both politics and period costuming.

It is an ugly costume, but it did make a fine background for the Order of Wilhelmina stretched in colorful diagonal across my chest. I looked at myself in a long glass and was pleased with the effect; the one color accent against the dead black and white was good showmanship. The traditional dress might be ugly but it did have dignity, something like the cool stateliness of a *maitre d'hôtel*. I decided that I looked the part to wait on the pleasure of a sovereign.

Rog Clifton gave me the scroll which was supposed to list the names of my nominations for the ministries and he tucked into an inner pocket of my costume a copy of the typed list thereof—the original had gone forward by hand of Jimmie Washington to the Emperor's State Secretary as soon as we had grounded. Theoretically the purpose of the audience was for the Emperor to inform me that it was his pleasure for me to form a government and for me to submit humbly my suggestions; my nominations were supposed to be secret until the sovereign graciously approved.

Actually the choices were all made; Rog and Bill had spent most of the trip lining up the Cabinet and making sure the nominees would serve, using state-scramble for the radio messages. I had studied the Farleyfiles on each nomination and each alternate. But the list really was secret in the sense that the news services would not receive it until after the Imperial audience.

I took the scroll and picked up my life wand. Rog looked horrified. "Good Lord, man, you can't carry that thing into the presence of the Emperor!"

"Why not?"

"Huh? It's a *weapon*."

"It's a ceremonial weapon. Rog, every duke and every pipsqueak baronet will be wearing his dress sword. So I wear this."

He shook his head. "They have to. Don't you understand the ancient legal theory behind it? Their dress swords symbolize the duty they owe their liege lord to support and defend him by force of arms, in their own persons. But you are a commoner; traditionally you come before him unarmed."

"No, Rog. Oh, I'll do what you tell me to, but you are missing a wonderful chance to catch a tide at its flood. This is good theater, this is *right.*"

"I'm afraid I don't follow you."

"Well, look, will the word get back to Mars if I carry this wand today? Inside the nests, I mean?"

"Eh? I suppose so. Yes."

"Of course. I would guess that every nest has stereo receivers; I certainly noticed plenty of them in Kkkah nest. They follow the Empire news as carefully as we do. Don't they?"

"Yes. At least the elders do."

"If I carry the wand, they'll know it; if I fail to carry it, they will know it. It matters to them; it is tied up with propriety. No adult Martian would appear outside his nest without his life wand, or inside on ceremonial occasions. Martians have appeared before the Emperor in the past; they carried their wands, didn't they? I'd bet my life on it."

"Yes, but you——"

"You forget that *I am a Martian.*"

Rog's face suddenly blanked out. I went on, "I am not only 'John Joseph Bonforte'; I am Kkkahjjjerrr of Kkkah nest. If I fail to carry that wand, I commit a great impropriety —and frankly I do not know what would happen when the word got back; I don't know enough about Martian customs. Now turn it around and look at it the other way. When I walk down that aisle carrying this wand, *I am a Martian citizen about to be named His Imperial Majesty's first minister.* How will that affect the nests?"

"I guess I had not thought it through," he answered slowly.

"Nor would I have done so, had I not had to decide whether or not to carry the wand. But don't you suppose Mr. B. thought it through—before he ever let himself be invited to be adopted? Rog, we've got a tiger by the tail; the only thing to do is to swarm aboard and ride it. We can't let go."

Dak arrived at that point, confirmed my opinion, seemed surprised that Clifton had expected anything else. "Sure, we're setting a new precedent, Rog—but we're going to set a lot of new ones before we are through." But when he saw how I was carrying the wand he let out a scream. "Cripes, man! Are you trying to kill somebody? Or just carve a hole in the wall?"

"I wasn't pressing the stud."

"Thank God for small favors! You don't even have the safety on." He took it from me very gingerly and said, "You twist this ring—and shove this in that slot—then it's just a stick. Whew!"

"Oh. Sorry."

They delivered me to the robing room of the Palace and turned me over to King Willem's equerry, Colonel Pateel, a bland-faced Hindu with perfect manners and the dazzling dress uniform of the Imperial space forces. His bow to me must have been calculated on a slide rule; it suggested that I was about to be Supreme Minister but was not quite there yet, that I was his senior but nevertheless a civilian—then subtract five degrees for the fact that he wore the Emperor's aiguillette on his right shoulder.

He glanced at the wand and said smoothly, "That's a Martian wand, is it not, sir? Interesting. I suppose you will want to leave it here—it will be safe."

I said, "I'm carrying it."

"Sir?" His eyebrows shot up and he waited for me to correct my obvious mistake.

I reached into Bonforte's favorite clichés and picked one he used to reprove bumptiousness. "Son, suppose you tend to your knitting and I tend to mine."

His face lost all expression. "Very well, sir. If you will come this way?"

We paused at the entrance to the throne room. Far away, on the raised dais, the throne was empty. On both sides the entire length of the great cavern the nobles and royalty of the court were standing and waiting. I suppose Pateel passed along some sign, for the Imperial Anthem welled out and we all held still for it, Pateel in robotlike attention, myself in a tired stoop suitable to a middle-aged and overworked man who must do this thing because he must, and all the court like show-window pieces. I hope we never dispense with the pageantry of a court entirely; all those noble dress extras and spear carriers make a beautiful sight.

In the last few bars he came in from behind and took his throne—Willem, Prince of Orange, Duke of Nassau, Grand Duke of Luxembourg, Knight Commander of the Holy Roman Empire, Admiral General of the Imperial Forces, Adviser to the Martian Nests, Protector of the Poor, and, by the Grace of God, King of the Lowlands and Emperor of the Planets and the Spaces Between.

I could not see his face, but the symbolism produced in me a sudden warm surge of empathy. I no longer felt hostile to the notion of royalty.

As King Willem sat down the anthem ended; he nodded

acknowledgment of the salute and a wave of slight relaxation rippled down the courtiers. Pateel withdrew and, with my wand tucked under my arm, I started my long march, limping a little in spite of the low gravity. It felt remarkably like the progress to the Inner Nest of Kkkah, except that I was not frightened; I was simply warm and tingling. The Empire medley followed me down, the music sliding from "Kong Christian" to "Marseillaise" to "The Star-Spangled Banner" and all the others.

At the first balk line I stopped and bowed, then again at the second, then at last a deep bow at the third, just before the steps. I did not kneel; nobles must kneel but commoners share sovereignty with the Sovereign. One sees this point incorrectly staged sometimes in stereo and theater, and Rog had made sure that I knew what to do.

"*Ave, Imperator!*" Had I been a Dutchman I would have said "Rex" as well, but I was an American. We swapped schoolboy Latin back and forth by rote, he inquiring what I wanted, I reminding him that he had summoned me, etc. He shifted into Anglo-American, with a slight "down-East" accent.

"You served our father well. It is now our thought that you might serve us. How say you?"

"My sovereign's wish is my will, Majesty."

"Approach us."

Perhaps I made too good a thing of it but the steps up the dais are high and my leg actually was hurting—and a psychosomatic pain is as bad as any other. I almost stumbled—and Willem was up out of his throne like a shot and steadied my arm. I heard a gasp go around the hall. He smiled at me and said *sotto voce*, "Take it easy, old friend. We'll make this short."

He helped me to the stool before the throne and made me sit down an awkward moment sooner than he himself was again seated. Then he held out his hand for the scroll and I passed it over. He unrolled it and pretended to study the blank page.

There was chamber music now and the court made a display of enjoying themselves, ladies laughing, noble gentlemen uttering gallantries, fans gesturing. No one moved very far from his place, no one held still. Little page boys, looking like Michelangelo's cherubim, moved among them offering trays of sweets. One knelt to Willem and he helped himself without taking his eyes off the nonexistent list. The child then offered the tray to me and I took one, not knowing whether it was proper or not. It was one of those wonderful, matchless chocolates made only in Holland.

I found that I knew a number of the court faces from

pictures. Most of the unemployed royalty of Earth were there, concealed under their secondary titles of duke or count. Some said that Willem kept them on as pensioners to brighten his court; some said he wanted to keep an eye on them and keep them out of politics and other mischief. Perhaps it was a little of both. There were the nonroyal nobility of a dozen nations present, too; some of them actually worked for a living.

I found myself trying to pick out the Habsburg lips and the Windsor nose.

At last Willem put down the scroll. The music and the conversation ceased instantly. In dead silence he said, "It is a gallant company you have proposed. We are minded to confirm it."

"You are most gracious, Majesty."

"We will ponder and inform you." He leaned forward and said quietly to me alone, "Don't try to back down those damned steps. Just stand up. I am going to leave at once."

I whispered back, "Oh. Thank you, Sire."

He stood up, whereupon I got hastily to my feet, and he was gone in a swirl of robes. I turned around and noticed some startled looks. But the music started up at once and I was let to walk out while the noble and regal extras again made polite conversation.

Pateel was at my elbow as soon as I was through the far archway. "This way, sir, if you please."

The pageantry was over; now came the real audience.

He took me through a small door, down an empty corridor, through another small door, and into a quite ordinary office. The only thing regal about it was a carved wall plaque, the coat of arms of the House of Orange, with its deathless motto, *"I Maintain!"* There was a big, flat desk, littered with papers. In the middle of it, held down by a pair of metal-plated baby shoes, was the original of the typed list in my pocket. In a copper frame there was a family group picture of the late Empress and the kids. A somewhat battered couch was against one wall and beyond it was a small bar. There were a couple of armchairs as well as the swivel chair at the desk. The other furnishings might have suited the office of a busy and not fussy family physician.

Pateel left me alone there, closing the door behind him. I did not have time to consider whether or not it was proper for me to sit down, as the Emperor came quickly in through a door opposite. "Howdy, Joseph," he called out. "Be with you in a moment." He strode through the room, followed closely by two servants who were undressing him as he walked, and went out a third door. He was back again almost at once, zipping up a suit of coveralls as he came in. "You took the short route; I had to come long way around. I'm going to insist that the palace engineer cut another tunnel through from the back of the throne room, damme if I'm not. I have to come around three sides of a square—either that or parade through semi-public corridors dressed like a circus horse." He added meditatively, "I never wear anything but underwear under those silly robes."

I said, "I doubt if they are as uncomfortable as this monkey jacket I am wearing, Sire."

He shrugged. "Oh well, we each have to put up with the inconveniences of our jobs. Didn't you get yourself a drink?" He picked up the list of nominations for cabinet ministers. "Do so, and pour me one."

"What will you have, Sire?"

"Eh?" He looked up and glanced sharply at me. "My usual. Scotch on ice, of course."

I said nothing and poured them, adding water to my own. I had had a sudden chill; if Bonforte knew that the Emperor always took scotch over bare cubes it should have been in his Farleyfile. It was not.

But Willem accepted the drink without comment, murmured, "Hot jets!" and went on looking at the list. Presently he looked up and said, "How about these lads, Joseph?"

"Sire? It is a skeleton cabinet, of course." We had doubled up on portfolios where possible and Bonforte would hold Defense and Treasury as well as first. In three cases we had given temporary appointments to the career deputy ministers—Research, Population Management, and Exterior. The men who would hold the posts in the permanent government were all needed for campaigning.

"Yes, yes, it's your second team. Mmm . . . How about this man Braun?"

I was considerably surprised. It had been my understanding that Willem would okay the list without comment, but that he might want to chat about other things. I had not been afraid of chatting; a man can get a reputation as a sparkling conversationalist simply by letting the other man do all the talking.

Lothar Braun was what was known as a "rising young statesman." What I knew about him came from his Farleyfile and from Rog and Bill. He had come up since Bonforte had been turned out of office and so had never had any cabinet post, but had served as caucus sergeant at arms and junior whip. Bill insisted that Bonforte had planned to boost him rapidly and that he should try his wings in the caretaker government; he proposed him for Minister of External Communications.

Rog Clifton had seemed undecided; he had first put down

the name of Angel Jesus de la Torre y Perez, the career subminister. But Bill had pointed out that if Braun flopped, now was a good time to find it out and no harm done. Clifton had given in.

"Braun?" I answered. "He's a coming young man. Very brilliant."

Willem made no comment, but looked on down the list. I tried to remember exactly what Bonforte had said about Braun in the Farleyfile. Brilliant . . . hardworking . . . analytical mind. Had he said anything against him? No—well, perhaps—"a shade too affable." That does not condemn a man. But Bonforte had said nothing at all about such affirmative virtues as loyalty and honesty. Which might mean nothing, as the Farleyfile was not a series of character studies; it was a data file.

The Emperor put the list aside. "Joseph, are you planning to bring the Martian nests into the Empire at once?"

"Eh? Certainly not before the election, Sire."

"Come now, you know I was talking about after the election. And have you forgotten how to say 'Willem'? 'Sire' from a man six years older than I am, under these circumstances, is silly."

"Very well, Willem."

"We both know I am not supposed to notice politics. But we know also that the assumption is silly. Joseph, you have spent your off years creating a situation in which the nests would wish to come wholly into the Empire." He pointed a thumb at my wand. "I believe you have done it. Now if you win this election you should be able to get the Grand Assembly to grant me permission to proclaim it. Well?"

I thought about it. "Willem," I said slowly, "you know that is exactly what we have planned to do. You must have some reason for bringing the subject up."

He swizzled his glass and stared at me, managing to look like a New England groceryman about to tell off one of the summer people. "Are you asking my advice? The constitution requires you to advise me, not the other way around."

"I welcome your advice, Willem. I do not promise to follow it."

He laughed. "You damned seldom promise anything. Very well, let's assume that you win the election and go back into office—but with a majority so small that you might have difficulty in voting the nests into full citizenship. In such case I would not advise you to make it a vote of confidence. If you lose, take your licking and stay in office; stick the full term."

"Why, Willem?"

"Because you and I are patient men. See that?" He pointed at the plaque of his house. " 'I Maintain!' It's not a flashy rule but it is not a king's business to be flashy; his business is to conserve, to hang on, to roll with the punch. Now, constitutionally speaking, it should not matter to me whether you stay in office or not. But it does matter to me whether or not the Empire holds together. I think that if you miss on the Martian issue immediately after the election, you can afford to wait—for your other policies are going to prove very popular. You'll pick up votes in by-elections and eventually you'll come around and tell me I can add 'Emperor of Mars' to the list. So don't hurry."

"I will think about it," I said carefully.

"Do that. Now how about the transportee system?"

"We're abolishing it immediately after the election and suspending it at once." I could answer that one firmly; Bonforte hated it.

"They'll attack you on it."

"So they will. Let them. We'll pick up votes."

"Glad to hear that you still have the strength of your convictions, Joseph. I never liked having the banner of Orange on a convict ship. Free trade?"

"After the election, yes."

"What are you going to use for revenue?"

"It is our contention that trade and production will expand so rapidly that other revenues will make up for the loss of the customs."

"And suppose it ain't so?"

I had not been given a second-string answer on that one—and economics was largely a mystery to me. I grinned. "Willem, I'll have to have notice on that question. But the whole program of the Expansionist Party is founded on the notion that free trade, free travel, common citizenship, common currency, and a minimum of Imperial laws and restrictions are good not only for the citizens of the Empire but for the Empire itself. If we need the money, we'll find it—but not by chopping the Empire up into tiny bailiwicks." All but the first sentence was pure Bonforte, only slightly adapted.

"Save your campaign speeches," he grunted. "I simply asked." He picked up the list again. "You're quite sure this line-up is the way you want it?"

I reached for the list and he handed it to me. Damnation, it was clear that the Emperor was telling me as emphatically as the constitution would let him that, in his opinion, Braun was a wrong 'un. But, hell's best anthracite, I had no business changing the list Bill and Rog had made up.

On the other hand, it was not *Bonforte's* list; it was merely

96

what they thought Bonforte would do if he were *compos mentis.*

I wished suddenly that I could take time out and ask Penny what she thought of Braun.

Then I reached for a pen from Willem's desk, scratched out "Braun," and printed in "de la Torre"—in block letters; I still could not risk Bonforte's handwriting. The Emperor merely said, "It looks like a good team to me. Good luck, Joseph. You'll need it."

That ended the audience as such. I was anxious to get away, but you do not walk out on a king; that is one prerogative they have retained. He wanted to show me his workshop and his new train models. I suppose he has done more to revive that ancient hobby than anyone else; personally I can't see it as an occupation for a grown man. But I made polite noises about his new toy locomotive, intended for the "Royal Scotsman."

"If I had had the breaks," he said, getting down on his hands and knees and peering into the innards of the toy engine, "I could have been a very fair shop superintendent, I think—a master machinist. But the accident of birth discriminated against me."

"Do you really think you would have preferred it, Willem?"

"I don't know. This job I have is not bad. The hours are easy and the pay is good—and the social security is first-rate—barring the outside chance of revolution, and my line has always been lucky on that score. But much of the work is tedious and could be done as well by any second-rate actor." He glanced up at me. "I relieve your office of a lot of tiresome cornerstone-laying and parade-watching, you know."

"I do know and I appreciate it."

"Once in a long time I get a chance to give a little push in the right direction—what I think is the right direction. Kinging is a very odd profession, Joseph. Don't ever take it up."

"I'm afraid it's a bit late, even if I wanted to."

He made some fine adjustment on the toy. "My real function is to keep you from going crazy."

"Eh?"

"Of course. Psychosis-situational is the occupational disease of heads of states. My predecessors in the king trade, the ones who actually ruled, were almost all a bit balmy. And take a look at your American presidents; the job used frequently to kill them in their prime. But me, I don't have to run things; I have a professional like yourself to do it for me. And you don't have the killing pressure either; you, or those in your shoes, can always quit if things get too tough

97

—and the old Emperor—it's almost always the 'old' Emperor; we usually mount the throne about the age other men retire —the Emperor is always there, maintaining continuity, preserving the symbol of the state, while you professionals work out a new deal." He blinked solemnly. "My job is not glamorous, but it *is* useful."

Presently he let up on me about his childish trains and we went back into his office. I thought I was about to be dismissed. In fact, he said, "I should let you get back to your work. You had a hard trip?"

"Not too hard. I spent it working."

"I suppose so. By the way, who *are* you?"

There is the policeman's tap on the shoulder, the shock of the top step that is not there, there is falling out of bed, and there is having her husband return home unexpectedly—I would take any combination of those in preference to that simple inquiry. I aged inside to match my appearance and more.

"Sire?"

"Come now," he said impatiently, "surely my job carries with it some privileges. Just tell me the truth. I've known for the past hour that you were not Joseph Bonforte— though you could fool his own mother; you even have his mannerisms. But who are you?"

"My name is Lawrence Smith, Your Majesty," I said faintly.

"Brace up, man! I could have called the guards long since, if I had been intending to. Were you sent here to assassinate me?"

"No, Sire. I am—loyal to Your Majesty."

"You have an odd way of showing it. Well, pour yourself another drink, sit down, and tell me about it."

I told him about it, every bit. It took more than one drink, and presently I felt better. He looked angry when I told him of the kidnaping, but when I told him what they had done to Bonforte's mind his face turned dark with a Jovian rage.

At last he said quietly, "It's just a matter of days until he is back in shape, then?"

"So Dr. Capek says."

"Don't let him go to work until he is fully recovered. He's a valuable man. You know that, don't you? Worth six of you and me. So you carry on with the doubling job and let him get well. The Empire needs him."

"Yes, Sire."

"Knock off that 'Sire.' Since you are standing in for him, call me 'Willem,' as he does. Did you know that was how I spotted you?"

"No, Si—no, Willem."

"He's called me Willem for twenty years. I thought it decidedly odd that he would quit it in private simply because he was seeing me on state business. But I did not suspect, not really. But, remarkable as your performance was, it set me thinking. Then when we went in to see the trains, I knew."

"Excuse me? How?"

"You were *polite*, man! I've made him look at my trains in the past—and he always got even by being as rude as possible about what a way for a grown man to waste time. It was a little act we always went through. We both enjoyed it."

"Oh. I didn't know."

"How could you have known?" I was thinking that I should have known, that damned Farleyfile should have told me . . . It was not until later that I realized that the file had not been defective, in view of the theory on which it was based, i.e. it was intended to let a famous man remember details about the *less* famous. But that was precisely what the Emperor was *not*—less famous, I mean. Of *course* Bonforte needed no notes to recall personal details about Willem! Nor would he consider it proper to set down personal matters about the sovereign in a file handled by his clerks.

I had muffed the obvious—not that I see how I could have avoided it, even if I had realized that the file would be incomplete.

But the Emperor was still talking. "You did a magnificent job—and after risking your life in a Martian nest I am not surprised that you were willing to tackle me. Tell me, have I ever seen you in stereo, or anywhere?"

I had given my legal name, of course, when the Emperor demanded it; I now rather timidly gave my professional name. He looked at me, threw up his hands, and guffawed. I was somewhat hurt. "Er, have you heard of me?"

"Heard of you? I'm one of your staunchest fans." He looked at me very closely. "But you still look like Joe Bonforte. I can't believe that you are Lorenzo."

"But I am."

"Oh, I believe it, I believe it. You know that skit where you are a tramp? First you try to milk a cow—no luck. Finally you end up eating out of the cat's dish—but even the cat pushes you away?"

I admitted it.

"I've almost worn out my spool of that. I laugh and cry at the same time."

"That is the idea." I hesitated, then admitted that the barnyard "Weary Willie" routine had been copied from a very great artist of another century. "But I prefer dramatic roles."

"Like this one?"

"Well—not exactly. For this role, once is quite enough. I wouldn't care for a long run."

"I suppose so. Well, tell Roger Clifton—— No, don't tell Clifton anything. Lorenzo, I see nothing to be gained by ever telling anyone about our conversation this past hour. If you tell Clifton, even though you tell him that I said not to worry, it would just give him nerves. And he has work to do. So we keep it tight, eh?"

"As my emperor wishes."

"None of that, please. We'll keep it quiet because it's best so. Sorry I can't make a sickbed visit on Uncle Joe. Not that I could help him—although they used to think the King's Touch did marvels. So we'll say nothing and pretend that I never twigged."

"Yes—Willem."

"I suppose you had better go now. I've kept you a very long time."

"Whatever you wish."

"I'll have Pateel go back with you—or do you know your way around? But just a moment——" He dug around in his desk, muttering to himself. "That girl must have been straightening things again. No—here it is." He hauled out a little book. "I probably won't get to see you again—so would you mind giving me your autograph before you go?"

9

Rog and Bill I found chewing their nails in Bonforte's upper living room. The second I showed up Corpsman started toward me. "Where the hell have you been?"

"With the Emperor," I answered coldly.

"You've been gone five or six times as long as you should have been."

I did not bother to answer. Since the argument over the speech Corpsman and I had gotten along together and worked together, but it was strictly a marriage of convenience, with no love. We co-operated, but we did not really bury the hatchet—unless it was between my shoulder blades. I had made no special effort to conciliate him and saw no reason why I should—in my opinion his parents had met briefly at a masquerade ball.

I don't believe in rowing with other members of the

company, but the only behavior Corpsman would willingly accept from me was that of a servant, hat in hand and very 'umble, sir. I would not give him that, even to keep peace. I was a professional, retained to do a very difficult professional job, and professional men do not use the back stairs; they are treated with respect.

So I ignored him and asked Rog, "Where's Penny?"

"With *him*. So are Dak and Doc, at the moment."

"He's here?"

"Yes." Clifton hesitated. "We put him in what is supposed to be the wife's room of your bedroom suite. It was the only place where we could maintain utter privacy and still give him the care he needs. I hope you don't mind."

"Not at all."

"It won't inconvenience you. The two bedrooms are joined, you may have noticed, only through the dressing rooms, and we've shut off that door. It's soundproof."

"Sounds like a good arrangement. How is he?"

Clifton frowned. "Better, much better—on the whole. He is lucid much of the time." He hesitated. "You can go in and see him, if you like."

I hesitated still longer. "How soon does Dr. Capek think he will be ready to make public appearances?"

"It's hard to say. Before long."

"How long? Three or four days? A short enough time that we could cancel all appointments and just put me out of sight? Rog, I don't know just how to make this clear but, much as I would like to call on him and pay my respects, I don't think it is smart for me to see him at all until after I have made my last appearance. It might well ruin my characterization." I had made the terrible mistake of going to my father's funeral; for years thereafter when I thought of him I saw him dead in his coffin. Only very slowly did I regain the true image of him—the virile, dominant man who had reared me with a firm hand and taught me my trade. I was afraid of something like that with Bonforte; I was now impersonating a well man at the height of his powers, the way I had seen him and heard him in the many stereo records of him. I was very much afraid that if I saw him ill, the recollection of it would blur and distort my performance.

"I was not insisting," Clifton answered. "You know best. It's possible that we can keep from having you appear in public again, but I want to keep you standing by and ready until he is fully recovered."

I almost said that the Emperor wanted it done that way. But I caught myself—the shock of having the Emperor find me out had shaken me a little out of character. But the thought reminded me of unfinished business. I took out the revised cabinet list and handed it to Corpsman. "Here's the approved roster for the news services, Bill. You'll see that there is one change on it—De la Torre for Braun."

"What?"

"Jesus de la Torre for Lothar Braun. That's the way the Emperor wanted it."

Clifton looked astonished; Corpsman looked both astonished and angry. "What difference does that make? He's got no goddamn right to have opinions!"

Clifton said slowly, "Bill is right, Chief. As a lawyer who has specialized in constitutional law I assure you that the sovereign's confirmation is purely nominal. You should not have let him make any changes."

I felt like shouting at them, and only the imposed calm personality of Bonforte kept me from it. I had had a hard day and, despite a brilliant performance, the inevitable disaster had overtaken me. I wanted to tell Rog that if Willem had not been a really big man, kingly in the fine sense of the word, we would all be in the soup—simply because I had not been adequately coached for the role. Instead I answered sourly, "It's done and that's that."

Corpsman said, "That's what *you* think! I gave out the correct list to the reporters two hours ago. Now you've got to go back and straighten it out. Rog, you had better call the Palace right away and——"

I said, "Quiet!"

Corpsman shut up. I went on in a lower key. "Rog, from a legal point of view, you may be right. I wouldn't know. I do know that the Emperor felt free to question the appointment of Braun. Now if either one of you wants to go to the Emperor and argue with him, that's up to you. But I'm not going anywhere. I'm going to get out of this anachronistic strait jacket, take my shoes off, and have a long, tall drink. Then I'm going to bed."

"Now wait, Chief." Clifton objected. "You've got a five-minute spot on grand network to announce the new cabinet."

"*You* take it. You're first deputy in this cabinet."

He blinked. "All right."

Corpsman said insistently, "How about Braun? He was promised the job."

Clifton looked at him thoughtfully. "Not in any dispatch that I saw, Bill. He was simply asked if he was willing to serve, like all the others. Is that what you meant?"

Corpsman hesitated like an actor not quite sure of his lines. "Of course. But it amounts to a promise."

"Not until the public announcement is made, it doesn't."

"But the announcement *was* made, I tell you. Two hours ago."

"Mmm . . . Bill, I'm afraid that you will have to call the boys in again and tell them that you made a mistake. Or I'll call them in and tell them that through an error a preliminary list was handed out before Mr. Bonforte had okayed it. But we've got to correct it before the grand network announcement."

"Do you mean to tell me you are going to let *him* get away with it?"

By "him" I think Bill meant me rather than Willem, but Rog's answer assumed the contrary. "Yes. Bill, this is no time to force a constitutional crisis. The issue isn't worth it. So will you phrase the retraction? Or shall I?"

Corpsman's expression reminded me of the way a cat submits to the inevitable—"just barely." He looked grim, shrugged, and said, "I'll do it. I want to be damned sure it is phrased properly, so we can salvage as much as possible out of the shambles."

"Thanks, Bill," Rog answered mildly.

Corpsman turned to leave. I called out, "Bill! As long as you are going to be talking to the news service I have another announcement for them."

"Huh? What are you after now?"

"Nothing much." The fact was I was suddenly overcome with weariness at the role and the tensions it created. "Just tell them that Mr. Bonforte has a cold and his physician has ordered him to bed for a rest. I've had a bellyful."

Corpsman snorted. "I think I'll make it 'pneumonia.' "

"Suit yourself."

When he had gone Rog turned to me and said, "Don't let it get you, Chief. In this business some days are better than others."

"Rog, I really am going on the sick list. You can mention it on stereo tonight."

"So?"

"I'm going to take to my bed and stay there. There is no reason at all why Bonforte can't 'have a cold' until he is ready to get back into harness himself. Every time I make an appearance it just increases the probability that somebody will spot something wrong—and every time I do make an appearance that sorehead Corpsman finds something to yap about. An artist can't do his best work with somebody continually snarling at him. So let's let it go at this and ring down the curtain."

"Take it easy, Chief. I'll keep Corpsman out of your hair from now on. Here we won't be in each other's laps the way we were in the ship."

"No, Rog, my mind is made up. Oh, I won't run out on you. I'll stay here until Mr. B. is able to see people, in case some utter emergency turns up"—I was recalling uneasily that the Emperor had told me to hang on and had assumed that I would—"but it is actually better to keep me out of sight. At the moment we have gotten away with it completely, haven't we? Oh, *they* know—somebody knows—that Bonforte was not the man who went through the adoption ceremony—but they don't dare raise that issue, nor could they prove it if they did. The same people may suspect that a double was used today, but they don't *know*, they can't be sure—because it is always possible that Bonforte recovered quickly enough to carry it off today. Right?"

Clifton got an odd, half-sheepish look on his face. "I'm afraid they are fairly sure you were a double, Chief."

"Eh?"

"We shaded the truth a little to keep you from being nervous. Doc Capek was certain from the time he first examined him that only a miracle could get him in shape to make the audience today. The people who dosed him would know that too."

I frowned. "Then you were kidding me earlier when you told me how well he was doing? How is he, Rog? Tell me the truth."

"I was telling you the truth that time, Chief. That's why I suggested that you see him—whereas before I was only too glad to string along with your reluctance to see him." He added, "Perhaps you had better see him, talk with him."

"Mmm—no." The reasons for not seeing him still applied; if I did have to make another appearance I did not want my subconscious playing me tricks. The role called for a well man. "But, Rog, everything I said applies still more emphatically on the basis of what you have just told me. If they are even reasonably sure that a double was used today, then we don't dare risk another appearance. They were caught by surprise today—or perhaps it was impossible to unmask me, under the circumstances. But it will not be later. They can rig some deadfall, some test that I can't pass—then *blooey!* There goes the old ball game." I thought about it. "I had better be 'sick' as long as necessary. Bill was right; it had better be 'pneumonia.'"

Such is the power of suggestion that I woke up the next morning with a stopped-up nose and a sore throat. Dr. Capek took time to dose me and I felt almost human by suppertime; nevertheless, he issued bulletins about "Mr. Bonforte's virus infection." The sealed and air-conditioned cities of the Moon being what they are, nobody was anxious to be exposed to an air-vectored ailment; no determined effort was made to get past my chaperones. For four days I loafed and read from Bonforte's library, both his own collected papers and his many books . . . I discovered that both politics and economics could make engrossing reading; those subjects had never been real to me before. The Emperor sent me flowers from the royal greenhouse—or were they for *me?*

Never mind. I loafed and soaked in the luxury of being Lorenzo, or even plain Lawrence Smith. I found that I dropped back into character automatically if someone came in, but I can't help that. It was not necessary; I saw no one but Penny and Capek, except for one visit from Dak.

But even lotus-eating can pall. By the fourth day I was as tired of that room as I had ever been of a producer's waiting room and I was lonely. No one bothered with me; Capek's visits had been brisk and professional, and Penny's visits had been short and few. She had stopped calling me "Mr. Bonforte."

When Dak showed up I was delighted to see him. "Dak! What's new?"

"Not much. I've been trying to get the *Tommie* overhauled with one hand while helping Rog with political chores with the other. Getting this campaign lined up is going to give him ulcers, three gets you eight." He sat down. "Politics!"

"Hmm . . . Dak, how did you ever get into it? Offhand, I would figure *voyageurs* to be as unpolitical as actors. And you in particular."

"They are and they aren't. Most ways they don't give a damn whether school keeps or not, as long as they can keep on herding junk through the sky. But to do that you've got to have cargo, and cargo means trade, and profitable trade means wide-open trade, with any ship free to go anywhere, no customs nonsense and no restricted areas. Freedom! And there you are; you're in politics. As for myself, I came here first for a spot of lobbying for the 'continuous voyage' rule, so that goods on the triangular trade would not pay two duties. It was Mr. B.'s bill, of course. One thing led to another and here I am, skipper of his yacht the past six years and representing my guild brothers since the last general election." He sighed. "I hardly know how it happened myself."

"I suppose you are anxious to get out of it. Are you going to stand for re-election?"

He stared at me. "Huh? Brother, until you've been in politics you haven't been *alive.*"

"But you said——"

"I know what I said. It's rough and sometimes it's dirty and it's always hard work and tedious details. But it's the only sport for grownups. All other games are for kids. All of 'em." He stood up. "Gotta run."

105

"Oh, stick around."

"Can't. With the Grand Assembly convening tomorrow I've got to give Rog a hand. I shouldn't have stopped in at all."

"It is? I didn't know." I was aware that the G.A., the outgoing G.A. that is, had to meet one more time, to accept the caretaker cabinet. But I had not thought about it. It was a routine matter, as perfunctory as presenting the list to the Emperor. "Is *he* going to be able to make it?"

"No. But don't you worry about it. Rog will apologize to the house for your—I mean *his*—absence and will ask for a proxy rule under no-objection procedure. Then he will read the speech of the Supreme Minister Designate—Bill is working on it right now. Then in his own person he will move that the government be confirmed. Second. No debate. Pass. Adjourn sine die—and everybody rushes for home and starts promising the voters two women in every bed and a hundred Imperials every Monday morning. Routine." He added, "Oh yes! Some member of the Humanity Party will move a resolution of sympathy and a basket of flowers, which will pass in a fine hypocritical glow. They'd rather send flowers to Bonforte's funeral." He scowled.

"It is actually as simple as that? What would happen if the proxy rule were refused? I thought the Grand Assembly didn't recognize proxies."

"They don't, for all ordinary procedure. You either pair, or you show up and vote. But this is just the idler wheels going around in parliamentary machinery. If they don't let him appear by proxy tomorrow, then they've got to wait around until he is well before they can adjourn sine die and get on with the serious business of hypnotizing the voters. As it is, a mock quorum has been meeting daily and adjourning ever since Quiroga resigned. This Assembly is as dead as Caesar's ghost, but it has to be buried constitutionally."

"Yes—but suppose some idiot *did* object?"

"No one will. Oh, it could force a constitutional crisis. But it won't happen."

Neither one of us said anything for a while. Dak made no move to leave. "Dak, would it make things easier if I showed up and gave that speech?"

"Huh? Shucks, I thought that was settled. You decided that it wasn't safe to risk another appearance short of an utter save-the-baby emergency. On the whole, I agree with you. There's the old saw about the pitcher and the well."

"Yes. But this is just a walk-through, isn't it? Lines as fixed as a play? Would there be any chance of anyone pulling any surprises on me that I couldn't handle?"

"Well, no. Ordinarily you would be expected to talk to

the press afterwards, but your recent illness is an excuse. We could slide you through the security tunnel and avoid them entirely." He smiled grimly. "Of course, there is always the chance that some crackpot in the visitors' gallery has managed to sneak in a gun . . . Mr. B. always referred to it as the 'shooting gallery' after they winged him from it."

My leg gave a sudden twinge. "Are you trying to scare me off?"

"No."

"You pick a funny way to encourage me. Dak, be level with me. Do you *want* me to do this job tomorrow? Or don't you?"

"Of course I do! Why the devil do you think I stopped in on a busy day? Just to chat?"

The Speaker pro tempore banged his gavel, the chaplain gave an invocation that carefully avoided any differences between one religion and another—and everyone kept silent. The seats themselves were only half filled but the gallery was packed with tourists.

We heard the ceremonial knocking amplified over the speaker system; the Sergeant at Arms rushed the mace to the door. Three times the Emperor demanded to be admitted, three times he was refused. Then he prayed the privilege; it was granted by acclamation. We stood while Willem entered and took his seat back of the Speaker's desk. He was in uniform as Admiral General and was unattended, as was required, save by escort of the Speaker and the Sergeant at Arms.

Then I tucked my wand under my arm and stood up at my place at the front bench and, addressing the Speaker as if the sovereign were not present, I delivered my speech. It was not the one Corpsman had written; that one went down the oubliette as soon as I had read it. Bill had made it a straight campaign speech, and it was the wrong time and place.

Mine was short, non-partisan, and cribbed right straight out of Bonforte's collected writings, a paraphrase of the one the time before when he formed a caretaker government. I stood foursquare for good roads and good weather and wished that everybody would love everybody else, just the way all us good democrats loved our sovereign and he loved us. It was a blank-verse lyric poem of about five hundred words and if I varied from Bonforte's earlier speech then I simply went up on my lines.

They had to quiet the gallery.

Rog got up and moved that the names I had mentioned in passing be confirmed—second and no objection and the clerk cast a white ballot. As I marched forward, attended by one member of my own party and one member of the opposition, I could see members glancing at their watches and wondering if they could still catch the noon shuttle.

Then I was swearing allegiance to my sovereign, under and subject to the constitutional limitations, swearing to defend and continue the rights and privileges of the Grand Assembly, and to protect the freedoms of the citizens of the Empire wherever they might be—and incidentally to carry out the duties of His Majesty's Supreme Minister. The chaplain mixed up the words once, but I straightened him out.

I thought I was breezing through it as easy as a curtain speech—when I found that I was crying so hard that I could hardly see. When I was done, Willem said quietly to me, "A good performance, Joseph." I don't know whether he thought he was talking to me or to his old friend—and I did not care. I did not wipe away the tears; I just let them drip as I turned back to the Assembly. I waited for Willem to leave, then adjourned them.

Diana, Ltd., ran four extra shuttles that afternoon. New Batavia was deserted—that is to say there were only the court and a million or so butchers, bakers, candlestick makers, and civil servants left in town—and a skeleton cabinet.

Having gotten over my "cold" and appeared publicly in the Grand Assembly Hall, it no longer made sense to hide out. As the supposed Supreme Minister I could not, without causing comment, never be seen; as the nominal head of a political party entering a campaign for a general election I had to see people—some people, at least. So I did what I had to do and got a daily report on Bonforte's progress toward complete recovery. His progress was good, if slow; Capek reported that it was possible, if absolutely necessary, to let him appear any time now—but he advised against it; he had lost almost twenty pounds and his co-ordination was poor.

Rog did everything possible to protect both of us. Mr. Bonforte knew now that they were using a double for him and, after a first fit of indignation, had relaxed to necessity and approved it. Rog ran the campaign, consulting him only on matters of high policy, and then passing on his answers to me to hand out publicly when necessary.

But the protection given me was almost as great; I was as hard to see as a topflight agent. My office ran on into the mountain beyond the opposition leader's apartments (we did not move over into the Supreme Minister's more palatial quarters; while it would have been legal, it just "was not done" during a caretaker regime)—they could not be reached from the rear directly from the lower living room, but to get at me from the public entrance a man had to pass about five check points—except for the favored few who were conducted directly by Rog through a bypass tunnel to Penny's office and from there into mine.

The setup meant that I could study the Farleyfile on anyone before he got to see me. I could even keep it in front of me while he was with me, for the desk had a recessed viewer the visitor could not see, yet I could wipe it out instantly if he turned out to be a floor pacer. The viewer had other uses; Rog could give a visitor the special treatment, rushing him right in to see me, leave him alone with me—and stop in Penny's office and write me a note, which would then be projected on the viewer—such quick tips as, "Kiss him to death and promise nothing," or, "All he really wants is for his wife to be presented at court. Promise him that and get rid of him," or even, "Easy on this one. It's a 'swing' district and he is smarter than he looks. Turn him over to me and I'll dicker."

I don't know who ran the government. The senior career men, probably. There would be a stack of papers on my desk each morning, I would sign Bonforte's sloppy signature to them, and Penny would take them away. I never had time to read them. The very size of the Imperial machinery dismayed me. Once when we had to attend a meeting outside the offices, Penny had led me on what she called a short cut through the Archives—miles on miles of endless files, each one chockablock with microfilm and all of them with moving belts scooting past them so that a clerk would not take all day to fetch one file.

But Penny told me that she had taken me through only one wing of it. The file of the files, she said, occupied a cavern the size of the Grand Assembly Hall. It made me glad that government was not a career with me, but merely a passing hobby, so to speak.

Seeing people was an unavoidable chore, largely useless since Rog, or Bonforte through Rog, made the decisions. My real job was to make campaign speeches. A discreet rumor had been spread that my doctor had been afraid that my heart had been strained by the "virus infection" and had advised me to stay in the low gravity of the Moon throughout the campaign. I did not dare risk taking the impersonation on a tour of Earth, much less make a trip to Venus; the Farleyfile system would break down if I attempted to mix with crowds, not to mention the unknown hazards of the Actionist goon squads—what I would babble with a minim dose of neodexocaine in the forebrain none of us liked to think about, me least of all.

Quiroga was hitting all continents on Earth, making his stereo appearances as personal appearances on platforms in front of crowds. But it did not worry Rog Clifton. He shrugged and said, "Let him. There are no new votes to be picked up by personal appearances at political rallies. All it does is wear out the speaker. Those rallies are attended only by the faithful."

I hoped that he knew what he was talking about. The campaign was short, only six weeks from Quiroga's resignation to the day he had set for the election before resigning, and I was speaking almost every day, either on a grand network with time shared precisely with the Humanity Party, or speeches canned and sent by shuttle for later release to particular audiences. We had a set routine; a draft would come to me, perhaps from Bill although I never saw him, and then I would rework it. Rog would take the revised draft away; usually it would come back approved—and once in a while there would be corrections made in Bonforte's handwriting, now so sloppy as to be almost illegible.

I never ad-libbed at all on those parts he corrected, though I often did on the rest—when you get rolling there is often a better, more alive way to say a thing. I began to notice the nature of his corrections; they were almost always eliminations of qualifiers—make it blunter, let 'em like it or lump it!

After a while there were fewer corrections. I was getting with it.

I still never saw him. I felt that I could not "wear his head" if I looked at him on his sickbed. But I was not the only one of his intimate family who was not seeing him; Capek had chucked Penny out—for her own good. I did not know it at the time. I did know that Penny had become irritable, absent-minded, and moody after we reached New Batavia. She got circles under her eyes like a raccoon—all of which I could not miss, but I attributed it to the pressure of the campaign combined with worry about Bonforte's health. I was only partly right. Capek spotted it and took action, put her under light hypnosis and asked her questions —then he flatly forbade her to see Bonforte again until I was done and finished and shipped away.

The poor girl was going almost out of her mind from visiting the sickroom of the man she hopelessly loved—then going straight in to work closely with a man who looked and talked and sounded just like him, but in good health. She was probably beginning to hate me.

Good old Doc Capek got at the root of her trouble, gave her helpful and soothing post-hypnotic suggestions, and kept her out of the sick room after that. Naturally I was not told about it at the time; it wasn't any of my business. But Penny perked up and again was her lovable, incredibly efficient self.

It made a lot of difference to me. Let's admit it; at least

110

twice I would have walked out on the whole incredible rat race if it had not been for Penny.

There was one sort of meeting I had to attend, that of the campaign executive committee. Since the Expansionist Party was a minority party, being merely the largest fraction of a coalition of several parties held together by the leadership and personality of John Joseph Bonforte, I had to stand in for him and peddle soothing syrup to those prima donnas. I was briefed for it with painstaking care, and Rog sat beside me and could hint the proper direction if I faltered. But it could not be delegated.

Less than two weeks before election day we were due for a meeting at which the safe districts would be parceled out. The organization always had thirty to forty districts which could be used to make someone eligible for cabinet office, or to provide for a political secretary (a person like Penny was much more valuable if he or she was fully qualified, able to move and speak on the floor of the Assembly, had the right to be present at closed caucuses, and so forth), or for other party reasons. Bonforte himself represented a "safe" district; it relieved him from the necessity of precinct campaigning. Clifton had another. Dak would have had one if he had needed it, but he actually commanded the support of his guild brethren. Rog even hinted to me once that if I wanted to come back in my proper person, I could say the word and my name would go on the next list.

Some of the spots were always saved for party wheel horses willing to resign at a moment's notice and thereby provide the Party with a place through a by-election if it proved necessary to qualify a man for cabinet office, or something.

But the whole thing had somewhat the flavor of patronage and, the coalition being what it was, it was necessary for Bonforte to straighten out conflicting claims and submit a list to the campaign executive committee. It was a last-minute job, to be done just before the ballots were prepared, to allow for late changes.

When Rog and Dak came in I was working on a speech and had told Penny to hold off anything but five-alarm fires. Quiroga had made a wild statement in Sydney, Australia, the night before, of such a nature that we could expose the lie and make him squirm. I was trying my hand at a speech in answer, without waiting for a draft to be handed me; I had high hopes of getting my own version approved.

When they came in I said, "Listen to this," and read them the key paragraph. "How do you like it?"

"That ought to nail his hide to the door," agreed Rog.

"Here's the 'safe' list, Chief. Want to look it over? We're due there in twenty minutes."

"Oh, that damned meeting. I don't see why I should look at the list. Anything you want to tell me about it?" Nevertheless, I took the list and glanced down it. I knew them all from their Farleyfiles and a few of them from contact; I knew already why each one had to be taken care of.

Then I struck the name: *Corpsman, William J.*

I fought down what I felt was justifiable annoyance and said quietly, "I see Bill is on the list, Rog."

"Oh, yes. I wanted to tell you about that. You see, Chief, as we all know, there has been a certain amount of bad blood between you and Bill. Now I'm not blaming you; it's been Bill's fault. But there are always two sides. What you may not have realized is that Bill has been carrying around a tremendous inferiority feeling; it gives him a chip on the shoulder. This will fix it up."

"So?"

"Yes. It is what he has always wanted. You see, the rest of us all have official status, we're members of the G.A., I mean. I'm talking about those who work closely around, uh, *you*. Bill feels it. I've heard him say, after the third drink, that he was just a hired man. He's bitter about it. You don't mind, do you? The Party can afford it and it's an easy price to pay for elimination of friction at headquarters."

I had myself under full control by now. "It's none of my business. Why should I mind, if that is what Mr. Bonforte wants?"

I caught just a flicker of a glance from Dak to Clifton. I added, "That *is* what Mr. B. wants? Isn't it, Rog?"

Dak said harshly, "Tell him, Rog."

Rog said slowly, "Dak and I whipped this up ourselves. We think it is for the best."

"Then Mr. Bonforte did not approve it? You asked him, surely?"

"No, we didn't."

"Why not?"

"Chief, this is not the sort of thing to bother him with. He's a tired, old, sick man. I have not been worrying him with anything less than major policy decisions—which this isn't. It is a district we command no matter who stands for it."

"Then why ask my opinion about it at all?"

"Well, we felt you should know—and know why. We think you ought to approve it."

"Me? You're asking me for a decision as if I were Mr. Bonforte. I'm not." I tapped the desk in his nervous gesture. "Either this decision is at his level, and you should ask *him*—or it's not, and you should never have asked *me*."

112

Rog chewed his cigar, then said, "All right, I'm not asking you."

"*No!*"

"What do you mean?"

"I mean 'No!' You did ask me; therefore there is doubt in your mind. So if you expect me to present that name to the committee—*as if* I were Bonforte—then go in and ask him."

They both sat and said nothing. Finally Dak sighed and said, "Tell the rest, Rog. Or I will."

I waited. Clifton took his cigar out of his mouth and said, "Chief, Mr. Bonforte had a stroke four days ago. He's in no shape to be disturbed."

I held still, and recited to myself all of "the cloud-capp'd towers, the gorgeous palaces," and so forth. When I was back in shape I said, "How is his mind?"

"His mind seems clear enough, but he is terribly tired. That week as a prisoner was more of an ordeal than we realized. The stroke left him in a coma for twenty-four hours. He's out of it now, but the left side of his face is paralyzed and his entire left side is partly out of service."

"Uh, what does Dr. Capek say?"

"He thinks that as the clot clears up, you'll never be able to tell the difference. But he'll have to take it easier than he used to. But, Chief, right now he is *ill*. We'll just have to carry on through the balance of the campaign without him."

I felt a ghost of the lost feeling I had had when my father died. I had never seen Bonforte, I had had nothing from him but a few scrawled corrections on typescript. But I leaned on him all the way. The fact that he was in that room next door had made the whole thing possible.

I took a long breath, let it out, and said, "Okay, Rog. We'll have to."

"Yes, Chief." He stood up. "We've got to get over to that meeting. How about *that?*" He nodded toward the safe-districts list.

"Oh." I tried to think. Maybe it was possible that Bonforte would reward Bill with the privilege of calling himself "the Honorable," just to keep him happy. He wasn't small about such things; he did not bind the mouths of the kine who tread the grain. In one of his essays on politics he had said, "I am not an intellectual man. If I have any special talent, it lies in picking men of ability and letting them work."

"How long has Bill been with him?" I asked suddenly.

"Eh? About four years. A little over."

Bonforte evidently had liked his work. "That's past one

113

general election, isn't it? Why didn't he make him an Assemblyman then?"

"Why, I don't know. The matter never came up."

"When was Penny put in?"

"About three years ago. A by-election."

"There's your answer, Rog."

"I don't follow you."

"Bonforte could have made Bill a Grand Assemblyman at any time. He didn't choose to. Change that nomination to a 'resigner.' Then if Mr. Bonforte wants Bill to have it, he can arrange a by-election for him later—when he's feeling himself."

Clifton showed no expression. He simply picked up the list and said, "Very well, Chief."

Later that same day Bill quit. I suppose Rog had to tell him that his arm-twisting had not worked. But when Rog told me about it I felt sick, realizing that my stiff-necked attitude had us all in acute danger. I told him so. He shook his head.

"But he knows it *all!* It was his scheme from the start. Look at the load of dirt he can haul over to the Humanity camp."

"Forget it, Chief. Bill may be a louse—I've no use for a man who will quit in the middle of a campaign; you just don't do that, ever. But he is not a rat. In his profession you don't spill a client's secrets, even if you fall out with him."

"I hope you are right."

"You'll see. Don't worry about it. Just get on with the job."

As the next few days passed I came to the conclusion that Rog knew Bill better than I did. We heard nothing from him or about him and the campaign went ahead as usual, getting rougher all the time, but with not a peep to show that our giant hoax was compromised. I began to feel better and buckled down to making the best Bonforte speeches I could manage—sometimes with Rog's help; sometimes just with his okay. Mr. Bonforte was steadily improving again, but Capek had him on absolute quiet.

Rog had to go to Earth during the last week; there are types of fence-mending that simply can't be done by remote control. After all, votes come from the precincts and the field managers count for more than the speechmakers. But speeches still had to be made and press conferences given; I carried on, with Dak and Penny at my elbow—of course I was much more closely with it now; most questions I could answer without stopping to think.

There was the usual twice-weekly press conference in the

offices the day Rog was due back. I had been hoping that he would be back in time for it, but there was no reason I could not take it alone. Penny walked in ahead of me, carrying her gear; I heard her gasp.

I saw then that Bill was at the far end of the table.

But I looked around the room as usual and said, "Good morning, gentlemen."

"Good morning, Mr. Minister!" most of them answered.

I added, "Good morning, Bill. Didn't know you were here. Whom are you representing?"

They gave him dead silence to reply. Every one of them knew that Bill had quit us—or had been fired. He grinned at me, and answered, "Good morning, *Mister Bonforte*. I'm with the Krein Syndicate."

I knew it was coming then; I tried not to give him the satisfaction of letting it show. "A fine outfit. I hope they are paying you what you are worth. Now to business—— The written questions first. You have them, Penny?"

I went rapidly through the written questions, giving out answers I had already had time to think over, then sat back as usual and said, "We have time to bat it around a bit, gentlemen. Any other questions?"

There were several. I was forced to answer "No comment" only once—an answer Bonforte preferred to an ambiguous one. Finally I glanced at my watch and said, "That will be all this morning, gentlemen," and started to stand up.

"Smythe!" Bill shouted.

I kept right on getting to my feet, did not look toward him.

"I mean you, Mr. Phony Bonforte-Smythe!" he went on angrily, raising his voice still more.

This time I did look at him, with astonishment—just the amount appropriate, I think, to an important official subjected to rudeness under unlikely conditions. Bill was pointing at me and his face was red. "You impostor! You small-time actor! You *fraud!*"

The London *Times* man on my right said quietly, "Do you want me to call the guard, sir?"

I said, "No. He's harmless."

Bill laughed. "So I'm harmless, huh? You'll find out."

"I really think I should, sir," the *Times* man insisted.

"No." I then said sharply, "That's enough, Bill. You had better leave quietly."

"Don't you wish I would?" He started spewing forth the basic story, talking rapidly. He made no mention of the kidnaping and did not mention his own part in the hoax, but implied that he had left us rather than be mixed up in any such swindle. The impersonation was attributed, correctly as

115

far as it went, to illness on the part of Bonforte—with a strong hint that we might have doped him.

I listened patiently. Most of the reporters simply listened at first, with that stunned expression of outsiders exposed unwillingly to a vicious family argument. Then some of them started scribbling or dictating into minicorders.

When he stopped I said, "Are you through, Bill?"

"That's enough, isn't it?"

"More than enough. I'm sorry, Bill. That's all, gentlemen. I must get back to work."

"Just a moment, Mr. Minister!" someone called out. "Do you want to issue a denial?" Someone else added, "Are you going to sue?"

I answered the latter question first. "No, I shan't sue. One doesn't sue a sick man."

"Sick, am I?" shouted Bill.

"Quiet down, Bill. As for issuing a denial, I hardly think it is called for. However, I see that some of you have been taking notes. While I doubt if any of your publishers would run this story, if they do, this anecdote may add something to it. Did you ever hear of the professor who spent forty years of his life proving that the *Odyssey* was not written by Homer—but by another Greek of the *same name?*"

It got a polite laugh. I smiled and started to turn away again. Bill came rushing around the table and grabbed at my arm. "You can't laugh it off!" The *Times* man—Mr. Ackroyd, it was—pulled him away from me.

I said, "Thank you, sir." Then to Corpsman I added, "What do you want me to do, Bill? I've tried to avoid having you arrested."

"Call the guards if you like, you phony! We'll see who stays in jail longest! *Wait until they take your fingerprints!*"

I sighed and made the understatement of my life. "This is ceasing to be a joke. Gentlemen, I think I had better put an end to this. Penny my dear, will you please have someone send in fingerprinting equipment?" I knew I was sunk—but, damn it, if you are caught by the Birkenhead Drill, the least you owe yourself is to stand at attention while the ship goes down. Even a villain should make a good exit.

Bill did not wait. He grabbed the water glass that had been sitting in front of me; I had handled it several times. "The hell with that! This will do."

"I've told you before, Bill, to mind your language in the presence of ladies. But you may keep the glass."

"You're bloody well right I'll keep it."

"Very well. Please leave. If not, I'll be forced to summon the guard."

He walked out. Nobody said anything. I said, "May I provide fingerprints for any of the rest of you?"

Ackroyd said hastily, "Oh, I'm sure we don't want them, Mr. Minister."

"Oh, by all means! If there is a story in this, you'll want to be covered." I insisted because it was in character—and in the second and third place, you can't be a little bit pregnant, or slightly unmasked—and I did not want my friends present to be scooped by Bill; it was the last thing I could do for them.

We did not have to send for formal equipment. Penny had carbon sheets and someone had one of those lifetime memo pads with plastic sheets; they took prints nicely. Then I said good morning and left.

We got as far as Penny's private office; once inside she fainted dead. I carried her into my office, laid her on the couch, then sat down at my desk and simply shook for several minutes.

Neither one of us was worth much the rest of the day. We carried on as usual except that Penny brushed off all callers, claiming excuses of some sort. I was due to make a speech that night and thought seriously of canceling it. But I left the news turned on all day and there was not a word about the incident of that morning. I realized that they were checking the prints before risking it—after all, I *was* supposed to be His Imperial Majesty's first minister; they would want confirmation. So I decided to make the speech since I had already written it and the time was scheduled. I couldn't even consult Dak; he was away in Tycho City.

It was the best one I had made. I put into it the same stuff a comic uses to quiet a panic in a burning theater. After the pickup was dead I just sunk my face in my hands and wept, while Penny patted my shoulder. We had not discussed the horrible mess at all.

Rog grounded at twenty hundred Greenwich, about as I finished, and checked in with me as soon as he was back. In a dull monotone I told him the whole dirty story; he listened, chewing on a dead cigar, his face expressionless.

At the end I said almost pleadingly, "I *had* to give the fingerprints, Rog. You see that, don't you? To refuse would not have been in character."

Rog said, "Don't worry."

"Huh?"

"I said, 'Don't worry.' When the reports on those prints come back from the Identification Bureau at The Hague, you are in for a small but pleasant surprise—and our ex-friend Bill is in for a much bigger one, but not pleasant. If he has collected any of his blood money in advance, they will probably take it out of his hide. I hope they do."

I could not mistake what he meant. "Oh! But, Rog—they won't stop there. There are a dozen other places. Social Security . . . Uh, lots of places."

"You think perhaps we were not thorough? Chief, I knew this could happen, one way or another. From the moment Dak sent word to complete Plan Mardi Gras, the necessary cover-up started. Everywhere. But I didn't think it necessary to tell Bill." He sucked on his dead cigar, took it out of his mouth, and looked at it. "Poor Bill."

Penny sighed softly and fainted again.

10

Somehow we got to the final day. We did not hear from Bill again; the passenger lists showed that he went Earthside two days after his fiasco. If any news service ran anything I did not hear of it, nor did Quiroga's speeches hint at it.

Mr. Bonforte steadily improved until it was a safe bet that he could take up his duties after the election. His paralysis continued in part but we even had that covered: he would go on vacation right after election, a routine practice that almost every politician indulges in. The vacation would be in the *Tommie,* safe from everything. Sometime in the course of the trip I would be transferred and smuggled back—and the Chief would have a mild stroke, brought on by the strain of the campaign.

Rog would have to unsort some fingerprints, but he could safely wait a year or more for that.

Election day I was happy as a puppy in a shoe closet. The impersonation was over, although I was going to do one more short turn. I had already canned two five-minute speeches for grand network, one magnanimously accepting victory, the other gallantly conceding defeat; my job was finished. When the last one was in the can, I grabbed Penny and kissed her. She didn't even seem to mind.

The remaining short turn was a command performance; Mr. Bonforte wanted to see me—as *him*—before he let me drop it. I did not mind. Now that the strain was over, it did not worry me to see him; playing him for his entertainment would be like a comedy skit, except that I would do it straight. What am I saying? Playing straight is the essence of comedy.

The whole family would gather in the upper living room—there because Mr. Bonforte had not seen the sky in some weeks and wanted to—and there we would listen to the returns, and either drink to victory or drown our sorrows and swear to do better next time. Strike me out of the last part; I had had my first and last political campaign and I wanted no more politics. I was not even sure I wanted to act again. Acting every minute for over six weeks adds up to about five hundred ordinary performances. That's a long run.

They brought him up the lift in a wheel chair. I stayed out of sight and let them arrange him on a couch before I came in; a man is entitled not to have his weakness displayed before strangers. Besides, I wanted to make an entrance.

I was almost startled out of character. He looked like my father! Oh, it was just a "family" resemblance; he and I looked much more alike than either one of us looked like my father, but the likeness was there—and the age was right, for he looked *old*. I had not guessed how much he had aged. He was thin and his hair was white.

I made an immediate mental note that during the coming vacation in space I must help them prepare for the transition, the resubstitution. No doubt Capek could put weight back on him; if not, there were ways to make a man appear fleshier without obvious padding. I would dye his hair myself. The delayed announcement of the stroke he had suffered would cover the inevitable discrepancies. After all, he *had* changed this much in only a few weeks; the need was to keep the fact from calling attention to the impersonation.

But these practical details were going on by themselves in a corner of my mind; my own being was welling with emotion. Ill though he was, the man gave off a force both spiritual and virile. I felt that warm, almost holy, shock one feels when first coming into sight of the great statue of Abraham Lincoln. I was reminded of another statue, too, seeing him lying there with his legs and his helpless left side covered with a shawl: the wounded Lion of Lucerne. He had that massive strength and dignity, even when helpless: "The guard dies, but never surrenders."

He looked up as I came in and smiled the warm, tolerant, and friendly smile I had learned to portray, and motioned with his good hand for me to come to him. I smiled the same smile back and went to him. He shook hands with a grip surprisingly strong and said warmly, "I am happy to meet you at last." His speech was slightly blurred and I could not see the slackness on the side of his face away from me.

"I am honored and happy to meet you, sir." I had to think about it to keep from matching the blurring of paralysis.

He looked me up and down, and grinned. "It looks to me as if you had already met me."

I glanced down at myself. "I have tried, sir."

" 'Tried'! You succeeded. It is an odd thing to see one's own self."

I realized with sudden painful empathy that he was not emotionally aware of his own appearance; my present appearance was "his"—and any change in himself was merely incidental to illness, temporary, not to be noticed. But he went on speaking. "Would you mind moving around a bit for me, sir? I want to see me—you—us. I want the audience's viewpoint for once."

So I straighened up, moved around the room, spoke to Penny (the poor child was looking from one to the other of us with a dazed expression), picked up a paper, scratched my collarbone and rubbed my chin, moved his wand from under my arm to my hand and fiddled with it.

He was watching with delight. So I added an encore. Taking the middle of the rug, I gave the peroration of one of his finest speeches, not trying to do it word for word, but interpreting it, letting it roll and thunder as he would have done—and ending with his own exact ending: "A slave cannot be freed, save he do it himself. Nor can you enslave a free man; the very most you can do is kill him!"

There was that wonderful hushed silence, then a ripple of clapping and Bonforte himself was pounding the couch with his good hand and calling, "Bravo!"

It was the only applause I ever got in the role. It was enough.

He had me pull up a chair then and sit with him. I saw him glance at the wand, so I handed it to him. "The safety is on, sir."

"I know how to use it." He looked at it closely, then handed it back. I had thought perhaps he would keep it. Since he did not, I decided to turn it over to Dak to deliver to him. He asked me about myself and told me that he did not recall ever seeing me play, but that he had seen my father's *Cyrano*. He was making a great effort to control the errant muscles of his mouth and his speech was clear but labored.

Then he asked me what I intended to do now. I told him that I had no plans as yet. He nodded and said, "We'll see. There is a place for you. There is work to be done." He made no mention of pay, which made me proud.

The returns were beginning to come in and he turned

his attention to the stereo tank. Returns had been coming in, of course, for forty-eight hours, since the outer worlds and the districtless constituencies vote before Earth does, and even on Earth an election "day" is more than thirty hours long, as the globe turns. But now we began to get the important districts of the great land masses of Earth. We had forged far ahead the day before in the outer returns and Rog had had to tell me that it meant nothing; the Expansionists always carried the outer worlds. What the billions of people still on Earth who had never been out and never would thought about it was what mattered.

But we needed every outer vote we could get. The Agrarian Party on Ganymede had swept five out of six districts; they were part of our coalition, and the Expanionist Party as such did not put up even token candidates. The situation on Venus was more ticklish, with the Venerians split into dozens of splinter parties divided on fine points of theology impossible for a human being to understand. Nevertheless, we expected most of the native vote, either directly or through caucused coalition later, and we should get practically all of the human vote there. The Imperial restriction that the natives must select human beings to represent them at New Batavia was a thing Bonforte was pledged to remove; it gained us votes on Venus; we did not know yet how many votes it would lose us on Earth.

Since the nests sent only observers to the Assembly the only vote we worried about on Mars was the Human vote. We had the popular sentiment; they had the patronage. But with an honest count we expected a shoo-in there.

Dak was bending over a slide rule at Rog's side; Rog had a big sheet of paper laid out in some complicated weighting formula of his own. A dozen or more of the giant metal brains through the Solar System were doing the same thing that night, but Rog preferred his own guesses. He told me once that he could walk through a district, "sniffing" it, and come within two per cent of its results. I think he could.

Doc Capek was sitting back, with his hands over his paunch, as relaxed as an angleworm. Penny was moving around, pushing straight things crooked and vice versa and fetching us drinks. She never seemed to look directly at either me or Mr. Bonforte.

I had never before experienced an election-night party; they were not like any other. There is a cozy, warm rapport of all passion spent. It really does not matter too much how the people decide; you have done your best, you are with your friends and comrades, and for a while there is no worry and no pressure despite the over-all excitement, like frosting on a cake, of the incoming returns.

I don't know when I've had so good a time.

Rog looked up, looked at me, then spoke to Mr. Bonforte. "The Continent is seesaw. The Americans are testing the water with a toe before coming in on our side; the only question is, how deep?"

"Can you make a projection, Rog?"

"Not yet. Oh, we have the popular vote but in the G.A. it could swing either way by half a dozen seats." He stood up. "I think I had better mosey out into town."

Properly speaking, I should have gone, as "Mr. Bonforte." The Party leader should certainly appear at the main headquarters of the Party sometime during election night. But I had never been in headquarters, it being the sort of a buttonholing place where my impersonation might be easily breached. My "illness" had excused me from it during the campaign; tonight it was not worth the risk, so Rog would go instead, and shake hands and grin and let the keyed-up girls who had done the hard and endless paperwork throw their arms around him and weep. "Back in an hour."

Even our little party should have been down on the lower level, to include all the office staff, especially Jimmie Washington. But it would not work, not without shutting Mr. Bonforte himself out of it. They were having their own party of course. I stood up. "Rog, I'll go down with you and say hello to Jimmie's harem."

"Eh? You don't have to, you know."

"It's the proper thing to do, isn't it? And it really isn't any trouble or risk." I turned to Mr. Bonforte. "How about it, sir?"

"I would appreciate it very much."

We went down the lift and through the silent, empty private quarters and on through my office and Penny's. Beyond her door was bedlam. A stereo receiver, moved in for the purpose, was blasting at full gain, the floor was littered, and everybody was drinking, or smoking, or both. Even Jimmie Washington was holding a drink while he listened to the returns. He was not drinking it; he neither drank nor smoked. No doubt someone had handed it to him and he had kept it. Jimmie had a fine sense of fitness.

I made the rounds, with Rog at my side, thanked Jimmie warmly and very sincerely, and apologized that I was feeling tired. "I'm going up and spread the bones, Jimmie. Make my excuses to people, will you?"

"Yes, sir. You've got to take care of yourself, Mr. Minister."

I went back up while Rog went on out into the public tunnels.

Penny shushed me with a finger to her lips when I came into the upper living room. Bonforte seemed to have dropped

122

off to sleep and the receiver was muted down. Dak still sat in front of it, filling in figures on the big sheet against Rog's return. Capek had not moved. He nodded and raised his glass to me.

I let Penny fix me a scotch and water, then stepped out into the bubble balcony. It was night both by clock and by fact and Earth was almost full, dazzling in a Tiffany spread of stars. I searched North America and tried to pick out the little dot I had left only weeks earlier, and tried to get my emotions straight.

After a while I came back in; night on Luna is rather overpowering. Rog returned a little later and sat back down at his work sheets without speaking. I noticed that Bonforte was awake again.

The critical returns were coming in now and everybody kept quiet, letting Rog with his pencil and Dak with his slide rule have peace to work. At long, long last Rog shoved his chair back. "That's it, Chief," he said without looking up. "We're in. Majority not less than seven seats, probably nineteen, possibly over thirty."

After a pause Bonforte said quietly, "You're sure?"

"Positive. Penny, try another channel and see what we get."

I went over and sat by Bonforte; I could not talk. He reached out and patted my hand in a fatherly way and we both watched the receiver. The first station Penny got said: "—doubt about it, folks; eight of the robot brains say yes, *Curiac* says maybe. The Expansionist Party has won a decisive——" She switched to another.

"—confirms his temporary post for another five years. Mr. Quiroga cannot be reached for a statement but his general manager in New Chicago admits that the present trend cannot be over——"

Rog got up and went to the phone; Penny muted the news down until nothing could be heard. The announcer continued mouthing; he was simply saying in different words what we already knew.

Rog came back; Penny turned up the gain. The announcer went on for a moment, then stopped, read something that was handed to him, and turned back with a broad grin. "Friends and fellow citizens, I now bring you for a statement the *Supreme Minister!*"

The picture changed to my victory speech.

I sat there luxuriating in it, with my feelings as mixed up as possible but all good, painfully good. I had done a job on the speech and I knew it; I looked tired, sweaty, and calmly triumphant. It sounded ad-lib.

I had just reached: "Let us go forward together, with freedom for all——" when I heard a noise behind me.

"Mr. Bonforte!" I said. "Doc! *Doc!* Come quickly!"

Mr. Bonforte was pawing at me with his right hand and trying very urgently to tell me something. But it was no use; his poor mouth failed him and his mighty indomitable will could not make the weak flesh obey.

I took him in my arms—then he went into Cheyne-Stokes breathing and quickly into termination.

They took his body back down in the lift, Dak and Capek together; I was no use to them. Rog came up and patted me on the shoulder, then he went away. Penny had followed the others down. Presently I went again out onto the balcony. I needed "fresh air" even though it was the same machine-pumped air as the living room. But it felt fresher.

They had killed him. His enemies had killed him as certainly as if they had put a knife in his ribs. Despite all that we had done, the risks we had taken, in the end they had murdered him. "Murder most foul"!

I felt dead inside me, numb with the shock. I had seen "myself" die, I had again seen my father die. I knew then why they so rarely manage to save one of a pair of Siamese twins. I was empty.

I don't know how long I stayed out there. Eventually I heard Rog's voice behind me. "Chief?"

I turned. "Rog," I said urgently, "don't call me that. Please!"

"Chief," he persisted, "you know what you have to do now? Don't you?"

I felt dizzy and his face blurred. I did not know what he was talking about—I did not *want* to know what he was talking about.

"What do you mean?"

"Chief—one man dies—but the show goes on. You can't quit now."

My head ached and my eyes would not focus. He seemed to pull toward me and away while his voice drove on. ". . . robbed him of his chance to finish his work. So you've got to do it for him. You've got to make him live again!"

I shook my head and made a great effort to pull myself together and reply. "Rog, you don't know what you are saying. It's preposterous—ridiculous! I'm no statesman. I'm just a bloody actor! I make faces and make people laugh. That's all I'm good for."

To my own horror I heard myself say it in Bonforte's voice.

Rog looked at me. "Seems to me you've done all right so far."

I tried to change my voice, tried to gain control of the situation. "Rog, you're upset. When you've calmed down you will see how ridiculous this is. You're right; the show goes on. But not that way. The proper thing to do—the *only* thing to do—is for you yourself to move on up. The election is won; you've got your majority—now you take office and carry out the program."

He looked at me and shook his head sadly. "I would if I could. I admit it. But I can't. Chief, you remember those confounded executive committee meetings? You kept them in line. The whole coalition has been kept glued together by the personal force and leadership of one man. If you don't follow through now, all that he lived for—and died for—will fall apart."

I had no answering argument; he might be right—I had seen the wheels within wheels of politics in the past month and a half. "Rog, even if what you say is true, the solution you offer is impossible. We've barely managed to keep up this pretense by letting me be seen only under carefully stage-managed conditions—and we've just missed being caught out as it is. But to make it work week after week, month after month, even year after year, if I understand you—no, it couldn't be done. It is impossible. I *can't* do it!"

"You *can!*" He leaned toward me and said forcefully, "We've all talked it over and we know the hazards as well as you do. But you'll have a chance to grow into it. Two weeks in space to start with—hell, a month if you want it! You'll study all the time—his journals, his boyhood diaries, his scrapbooks, you'll soak yourself in them. And we'll all help you."

I did not answer. He went on, "Look, Chief, you've learned that a political personality is not one man; it's a team—it's a team bound together by common purposes and common beliefs. We've lost our team captain and we've got to have another one. But the team is still there."

Capek was out on the balcony; I had not seen him come out. I turned to him. "Are you for this too?"

"Yes."

"It's your duty," Rog added.

Capek said slowly, "I won't go that far. I hope you will do it. But, damn it, I won't be your conscience. I believe in free will, frivolous as that may sound from a medical man." He turned to Clifton. "We had better leave him alone, Rog. He knows. Now it's up to him."

But, although they left, I was not to be alone just yet.

Dak came out. To my relief and gratitude he did not call me "Chief."

"Hello, Dak."

"Howdy." He was silent for a moment, smoking and looking out at the stars. Then he turned to me. "Old son, we've been through some things together. I know you now, and I'll back you with a gun, or money, or fists any time, and never ask why. If you choose to drop out now, I won't have a word of blame and I won't think any the less of you. You've done a noble best."

"Uh, thanks, Dak."

"One more word and I'll smoke out. Just remember this: if you decide you can't do it, the foul scum who brainwashed him will win. In spite of everything, they win." He went inside.

I felt torn apart in my mind—then I gave way to sheer self-pity. It wasn't fair! I had my *own* life to live. I was at the top of my powers, with my greatest professional triumphs still ahead of me. It wasn't right to expect me to bury myself, perhaps for years, in the anonymity of another man's role—while the public forgot me, producers and agents forgot me—would probably believe I was dead.

It wasn't fair. It was too much to ask.

Presently I pulled out of it and for a time did not think. Mother Earth was still serene and beautiful and changeless in the sky; I wondered what the election-night celebrations there sounded like. Mars and Jupiter and Venus were all in sight, strung like prizes along the zodiac. Ganymede I could not see, of course, nor the lonely colony out on far Pluto.

"Worlds of Hope," Bonforte had called them.

But he was dead. He was gone. They had taken away from him his birthright at its ripe fullness. He was dead.

And they had put it up to me to re-create him, make him live again.

Was I up to it? Could I possibly measure up to his noble standards? What would he want me to do? If he were in my place—what would Bonforte do? Again and again in the campaign I had asked myself: "What would Bonforte do?"

Someone moved behind me, I turned and saw Penny. I looked at her and said, "Did they send you out? Did you come to plead with me?"

"No."

She added nothing and did not seem to expect me to answer, nor did we look at each other. The silence went on. At last I said, "Penny? If I try to do it—will you help?"

She turned suddenly toward me. "Yes. Oh yes, Chief! I'll help!"

"Then I'll try," I said humbly.

I wrote all of the above twenty-five years ago to try to straighten out my own confusion. I tried to tell the truth and not spare myself because it was not meant to be read by anyone but myself and my therapist, Dr. Capek. It is strange, after a quarter of a century, to reread the foolish and emotional words of that young man. I remember him, yet I have trouble realizing that I was ever he. My wife Penelope claims that she remembers him better than I do—and that she never loved anyone else. So time changes us.

I find I can "remember" Bonforte's early life better than I remember my actual life as that rather pathetic person, Lawrence Smith, or—as he liked to style himself—"The Great Lorenzo." Does that make me insane? Schizophrenic, perhaps? If so, it is a necessary insanity for the role I have had to play, for in order to let Bonforte live again, that seedy actor had to be suppressed—completely.

Insane or not, I am aware that he once existed and that I was he. He was never a success as an actor, not really—though I think he was sometimes touched with the true madness. He made his final exit still perfectly in character; I have a yellowed newspaper clipping somewhere which states that he was "found dead" in a Jersey City hotel room from an overdose of sleeping pills—apparently taken in a fit of despondency, for his agent issued a statement that he had not had a part in several months. Personally, I feel that they need not have mentioned that about his being out of work; if not libelous, it was at least unkind. The date of the clipping proves, incidentally, that he would not have been in New Batavia, or anywhere else, during the campaign of '15.

I suppose I should burn it.

But there is no one left alive today who knows the truth other than Dak and Penelope—except the men who murdered Bonforte's body.

I have been in and out of office three times now and perhaps this term will be my last. I was knocked out the first time when we finally put the eetees—Venerians and Martians and Outer Jovians—into the Grand Assembly. But the non-human peoples are still there and I came back. The people will take a certain amount of reform, then they want a rest. But the reforms stay. People don't really want change, any change at all—and xenophobia is very deep-rooted. But we progress, as we must—if we are to go out to the stars.

Again and again I have asked myself: "What would Bonforte do?" I am not sure that my answers have always been right (although I am sure that I am the best-read student in his works in the System). But I have tried to stay in character in his role. A long time ago someone—Voltaire?—someone said, "If Satan should ever replace God he would find it necessary to assume the attributes of Divinity."

I have never regretted my lost profession. In a way, I have not lost it; Willem was right. There is other applause besides handclapping and there is always the warm glow of a good performance. I have tried, I suppose, to create the perfect work of art. Perhaps I have not fully succeeded—but I think my father would rate it as a "good performance."

No, I do not regret it, even though I was happier then—at least I slept better. But there is solemn satisfaction in doing the best you can for eight billion people.

Perhaps their lives have no cosmic significance, but they have feelings. They can hurt.